Airship 27 Productions

California Wolves

Published by Airship 27 Productions
www.airship27.com
www.airship27hangar.com

Editor: Ron Fortier
Associate Editor: Jonathan Sweet
Marketing and Promotions Manager: Michael Vance
Production Designer: Rob Davis

ISBN: 978-1-969285-12-7

Produced in the United States of America

10 9 8 7 6 5 4 3 2 1

CALIFORNIA WOLVES

(A BIGFOOT DETECTIVE NOVEL)

BY MICHAEL PANUSH

Redwood Jungle

Bigfoots (or bigfeet—either works) have big appetites.

Mine includes a taste for trouble.

This time, it came in the form of a bake sale as I was picking up my nephew from his elementary school. I noticed it when I cruised into the cement parking lot outside Sarsaparilla Springs Elementary, all set up in a little booth with a big banner above a folding card table that proved this wasn't the PTA. The sign had been done in crayon and sharpie—a big electric yellow circle with a pair of dark Xs in the middle, above the words 'Jefferson Rangers' and two spiky crossed rifles.

I'd heard the name of the outfit. It was a local club for humans, but I didn't know much more than that. Sasquatches have different social circles.

But they had cinnamon buns, brownies, and lemon squares for sale—and I've got a major sweet tooth.

Back in the day, when I grew up in the forest, the sweetest thing I tasted were the drippings of sap from the trunks of trees and whatever I could swipe from campsites. I'd spent much of my youth sneaking into tents and trailers, making off with whatever I could get my hands on, and a candy bar or a pack of cookies were a prime target.

Now, I just handed over cash like everyone else.

I was making my way over when the last bell rang and the kids came bounding out, a tide of sticky hands and bouncing backpacks. Schoolyard smells washed over the parking lot. Scented markers and sugary snacks, including—in open defiance of the 'peanut-free campus' sign by the main gate—some Reese's Peanut Butter Cups. Engines started rumbling to life as kids popped into car seats for the ride home.

I waved to my nephew, a furry speck amongst the tide of human children. "Milo! Your dad's got some police business over by Grizzly Hill, so he sent me to pick you up. I'm to watch you until your mom's afternoon class is over. Feel like a treat, furball?"

He sprang over. "Uncle Arlo—Joaquin said he saw a wolf outside his house." Milo had a blue polo shirt, his fur a shade lighter than mine. He was as excited as only a fourth grader with news to share could be. "Ms. Perry said it was a coyote, but Joaquin said he knows what coyotes are and this was much larger. We think it was a Gray Wolf, like they have in Oregon."

"A wolf." I hummed softly as we joined the line of parents perusing the baked goods. Wolves were gone from the forests of Northern California, just like so many other animals. Driven to extinction. Another entry on a long list of all the damage mankind had inflicted on the Holy Woods. "Couldn't be. You know what I think it was?"

"What?"

I grinned at him, showing off my fangs. "A extremely fat dog."

He rolled his eyes. What's the point of being an uncle if you can't be goofy?

One Ranger with a tight beard and a baseball cap slid in front of us as I was examining the snickerdoodles. "See anything you like?"

I eyeballed the Rangers. They lounged on folding chairs, sporting expensive shooting vests with patches that matched the flag, ball caps, overcomplicated holsters, and plenty of other expensive accessories that probably had 'tactical' in the description.

Halloween wasn't for another couple weeks, but these clowns were already in costume.

Milo gave him a polite nod. "Hello, Mr. Candle." His parents had instructed him well.

"Hello, buddy. This is your uncle?"

I offered my hands. "Arlo Patches. Good to meet you."

Milo picked up a box of blondies and gave it a sniff. "He's Caitlin's dad."

"That's right. And I own Candlewick Ranch, outside of town." A tall dude—for a human. Nearly tall enough to look me in the eye. Regular beanpole too, his plate carrier loose on his bantam-weight belly.

"Caitlin." I searched my memory. "They worked on the same science project last year."

The kids had been testing out different types of birdfeeders in the forest. I had watched Milo shimmy up trees with the fearlessness of a third grader and then tried to help his group write down all the complicated, far too long names for different birds that showed up for an easy snack.

I cracked a smile. "I helped him out with that one. Caitlin—she kept them in line without stepping on any toes. No easy feat."

He lit up with pride—happy as a buck showing off his antlers. For a second, he was just a dad, proud of his daughter—and then he was a Jefferson Ranger again. "Look, Arlo, I'm the Grand Marshall of the Nugget County Battalion of the Jefferson Rangers. We're recruiting for our coyote patrol—"

"Coyote patrol?"

All the good will vanished. My nostrils flared. Coyotes were one of the few animals who had the gumption to find a place for themselves in the human world. Before we left the woods, we'd learned to live with coyotes, and every other predator—respect them, give them space, understand that they were part of the Holy Woods. Humans would just reach for their weapons, with this Coyote Patrol being a perfect example.

Milo's talk about wolves had been the trigger, and Candle was pulling it.

I folded my arms. "You mean you kill the coyotes? Shoot them down?"

He shrank back. "To protect our herds. Most of us are ranchers." He motioned to the fliers on the booth, depicting a crossed-out coyote.

I hadn't noticed. Too focused on the treats.

Looks like my appetite had gotten me into trouble yet again.

I reached over and tapped the flyer. "You shoot them and celebrate, huh? Gun them down and break out the beers. Is that right?"

Most bigfeet aren't raging beasts, despite what some humans would have you believe. My brother Harold, Milo's dad, for instance, would have been smart enough to walk away. That's probably why he was respectable and so successful that he was the first bigfoot sheriff of Nugget County and I was, well, me.

Candle offered a sad smile. "Look, man, I know bigfoots—bigfeet—care about animals, but coyotes are a threat to my stock, not to mention kids and pets." He swallowed. "We don't hurt any that we don't have to." I'll bet. "The patrols are just part of it. We're just sticking up for the well-being of the common folk in Sarsaparilla Springs and throughout Northern California, and—"

"The common folk." A little October wind stirred my fur and tickled my skin. Carried a little sour fear from Candle. Fear of embarrassment—his pals were watching. It was gonna get worse. "What's that mean?"

"Uncle Arlo—" Milo tugged my arm. "Let's get these cookies and go—"

But Candle kept going. "Well, you and me, Arlo. You're country, like us. Folks in Sacramento don't care about the rural population, whether we got fur on our skin or not—" Holy Woods—of all the animals in the world, humans take the prize for sheer stubbornness. And stupidity.

I grunted loudly, flaring my nostrils. Opening my mouth to show my fangs too. Made a big bigfoot noise. It usually scared humans and it did now, making Candle step back until his hip bumped into the card table. Milo looked at me in horror and let out a nervous whimper.

But I kept going. "I'm not like you." Another insult, in the growling language of the Children, curdled in the back of my mind. *Harrower.* But if I called him that, he wouldn't have gotten it. "Keep playing in the woods, Mr. Grand Marshal. Have fun."

The other Rangers exchanged glances, clearly worried. Looking at Candle—their leader—who was doing his best dying fish impression as I stared him down. One of his pals, a plump Ranger in wraparound Oakleys, came around the table. He faced me—and Milo—and squared up. "Come on, man. We just want to be left alone. Isn't that why you and your furry friends stayed hidden in the forest all these years?" He had a 'Sergeant-at-Arms' patch perched on one side of his thick belly and 'Jerome' on the other. "Or maybe you're nothing but an animal." His eyes flicked to Milo. "You and li'l Fuzzy Wuzzy both."

Insulting Milo. He was about to find out why my Child's name is Porcupine. "We stayed in the woods because we wanted to be left alone, but now we're out of it." I got it for one reason—my temper. The Sacred Trees only know how much trouble my spines have gotten me into. "Because you and your species ruin everything you touch."

And here came some more.

A little axe rested on a stack of fliers. A paperweight. It had a sleek stealth-black finish and a half-moon blade. Jerome was looking at it, his fingers twitching. Was he gonna go for it? With Milo close by, I couldn't take the chance.

I moved first, got the grip of the axe, and hoisted it up.

"What in the woods' name is this?" The weapon was a toy in my hands. "You chopping down trees?"

Jerome sputtered. He'd overplayed his hand. "That's a tactical tomahawk."

The other Rangers looked on in horror. Not surprising. They were middle-class farmers and ranchers, like Candle. Spent their days dealing with nothing worse than an irate sheep, hawking their upscale wares to fancy artisanal shops. Then they bought expensive guns, gave themselves funny militaristic names, and thought themselves scary.

I had run with bank robbers, meth heads, and starving coyotes.

I knew scary.

I pushed Jerome back. Knocked him into the table. Gave the tomahawk a little spin and smashed the axe down, past him and into the clipboard resting by the fliers. Sundered the clipboard—and drove it deep enough in the flimsy plastic so that the half-moon blade jabbed out through the bottom and the handle stuck up like that magic sword in the King Arthur flicks beside the boxes of brownies.

"And I don't want to buy a lemon square either," I added.

Silence from the Rangers. Other parents—a small crowd of them—watched in stunned silence, a few going for their phones—though too scared or shocked to actually start dialing up the police. Candle bristled. He'd left his seat, taking a step toward his car. Probably had a gun rack inside.

The two of us faced off. Old school gunslingers—or a pair of bobcats squaring off over territory.

"Milo?" A little girl's voice. We looked up to see Caitlin, peeling off from a cluster of her friends and hurrying to the bake sale. She had her hair cut short and so pale it was nearly silver and wore a sweater with a leaping unicorn on it.

She stood next to Milo, who looked miserable.

When I saw the cub and the girl standing together, all the anger rushed out of me. The spell was broken. My face burned. Losing my temper—especially in front of some ranchers who were just trying to make a friend—was bad. Smashing up their table with an axe—sorry, tactical tomahawk—was even worse. And doing it in front of my nephew and his schoolyard pal? It was a regular forest fire of bad choices.

I had to get out of there.

"Uncle Arlo!" Milo hissed at me, as Caitlin advanced on her dad. "What are you doing?"

"Leaving, furball." I motioned to the pick-up. "Come on."

Caitlin looked from her dad and his friends to me, putting everything together.

Candle offered a smile, equal parts reassuring and sad. "Everything's okay, honey. Just a little disagreement. Adults argue sometimes."

"Is that what this was, daddy?" She stared at Milo as her dad withered like she was a miniature teacher, unraveling what had gone wrong in the school yard.

Milo stared at her, eyes big as a raccoon caught in the act of thievery. He didn't say anything.

I took hold of the cub's shoulder, stirring him toward the car. "Let's go, furball."

He shrugged me off. Writhed like a trapped rodent—twisting around and waving a fuzzy hand. "Goodbye, Caitlin! I'm sorry!"

"Bye, Milo!" She waved back. "It wasn't your fault!"

She was right about that.

I felt bad about it. One time, when I was Milo's age, I ignored my brother's warnings and snuck into a human campsite. Stole a whole cooler's worth of soda, which I hid in a hollow stump and guzzled during foraging sessions. The bubbles filled my belly, tickling and thick and making gas grow—until they burst forth in a series of burps and farts as big as bear roars to give me away. I got in all the trouble I had coming to me, and more still for lying. That's what guilt was like, and I had plenty. Losing my temper in front of Milo, embarrassing myself—that made it worse.

So I made it up to him with fast food.

We stopped at the McDonalds by the freeway entrance, away from downtown Sarsaparilla Springs with its cutesy tourist shops. We ate off their new Squatch Menu—all vegetarian. A Happy Meal—complete with toy—for Milo, while I got a trio of Double-Patty Bigfoot Burgers with extra cheese and spicy sauce, an order of Veggie Nuggets, and some fries. Would have liked to score one of their shakes too, but I wasn't that hungry.

Milo and I grabbed a table. Soda-stained floors left our feet sticky and the whole place stank of fry oil. It was wonderful. "I'm sorry." I pinched a mass of fries and tossed them in my mouth. "Just want to say that. You shouldn't lose your temper. Get into trouble—like I did."

He listened carefully. "Ms. Perry's very much against fighting. Two kids in my class were doing it and they had to write apology notes and missed an entire recess—and they both got phone calls home. If someone is being rude, we're supposed to tell them to stop and then tell an adult if they don't." He hesitated. Eyes downcast with disappointment and confusion. "Adults don't do that, though."

"Nah." I shrugged. "And I know Caitlin's your friend. I'm sure her dad's a nice guy. But what he's doing—with those Rangers—it gets under my fur."

"Caitlin says they get to carry guns." He seemed happy at the prospect.

"Your dad does too—and it's even better, because he's the sheriff." I took a big slurp of my Dr. Pepper. Now, I could drink all the soda I wanted and not feel guilty. The wonders of the human world. "The Rangers don't like laws." I couldn't say I cared for the law myself, especially considering that I'd broken the ones against bank robbery, assault, and grand theft auto a couple years back. "Well, maybe that's not such a bad thing, but they don't like environmental laws. You know. About where they can hunt, where they can fish, what rules they have to follow for their farms. What your Aunt Harriet's trying to do in Sacramento with the Sasquatch Political Action Committee."

The reason all of us had left the forest in the first place.

On the other hand, I hadn't exactly done my part for the forests and the earth.

Milo listened carefully as he chomped into his burger. "Caitlin says her dad inherited Candlewick Ranch from her grandfather, but it's tough to run. Seems like he's having a hard time keeping it going."

He had a heart open to everything, from the birds in the trees to sheep ranchers in the clearing. I gave him a quick smile. "Everything's hard in the human world, furball." My phone buzzed. I pulled it out. Sheriff Harold Patches—my big bro and Milo's dad. "I gotta take this. Why don't you open your toy, see what it is." I fiddled with the phone—the touchscreen too small for bigfoot fingers. Finally got it going. "Howdy, Harold."

His voice crept over the phone. Warm, deep—rich as summer thunder before a welcome storm. "Hi there, Arlo. Milo there?"

I spun the phone around, aiming the speaker at Milo. "Hi, dad!" Milo called.

"Nice to hear you, bud. Being good?"

I brought the phone back. "Definitely. Giving him a treat right now." He was tearing open the plastic packaging with his little fangs. I didn't want to mention fast food—his mom wouldn't approve. Decided to change the subject instead. "How's work? Any luck?"

"Folks around Grizzly Hill—I don't know. Tricky." Grizzly Hill was an outlaw haven. Meth and Fent Capitol of Northern California. Tricky was an understatement. "It's guns today. Chasing a shipment of some nasty firearms." I knew all about that sort of thing, but I didn't mention it. Didn't mention the Jefferson Rangers either. "I appreciate you looking after Milo, Arlo."

"It's no problem. I'll take him back to my place for the afternoon, maybe take in a movie." Something with lots of gunfire and explosions. I'd swear him to secrecy about the rating. Didn't want to make his parents mad. "It'll be fun."

"Actually, got something for your business."

"Business?" He could hear the reluctance in the hum following my words. The squeal of a fox pulled from the den.

"The thing about being a private investigator, Arlo, is that you have to investigate."

"Yeah, yeah." And, truth be told, I needed the job. Rent was coming due at the end of the month and fast food didn't pay for itself. "So what is it?"

"Gold mine, little brother. Missing Persons case, and the client's a major businessman by the name of Walter Rose. Runs the Rose Petal Winery down in Terroir Valley, along with quite a few other businesses. Major player in real estate. He's been calling the Sheriff's Department about a problem that's not really in our purview, but I told him I'd send him someone I trust. You should swing by within the hour. I'll text you the address."

"I'm honored, Squirrel." Using his Children's name.

"You being sarcastic, Porcupine?"

"Not that I know of, sheriff." I looked at the meal. "What about Milo?"

"Milo's a polite young sasquatch. It's not him I'm worried about. You play nice, okay?"

"I always do."

Chortling laughter from Harold. "All right, gotta go. See you soon. Walk peacefully under those sacred boughs, Arlo."

"You too." I hung up and looked at Milo. He held a cheap plastic toy—a simian critter with big white hands in a sailor suit outfit. When he pressed a button on the back, the hands—each fused in a two-fingered Peace Sign—jolted up and down. "What's that from?"

"Anime, I think. Happy Happy Hibagon Academy." He grinned, happy to play the professor. "Some of the older kids have told me about it. The show's about a human who enrolls at a school full of Hibagons—they're Japanese bigfeet—and has to pretend he's one too, to fit in. He ends up joining the Hibagon Yakuza and—"

"Anime—is that, like, cartoons?"

"Japanese animation, uncle."

"Uh-huh. How'd you get so smart?" I stood, popping open the plastic lid of the soda and sending the remaining Dr. Pepper and half-melted ice chunks down my throat. "Well, take the Hibagon on the road. We're going on a field trip."

"To Terroir Valley?"

"It's rude to eavesdrop, furball."

"It's rude to grab tomahawks and smash them into tables too."

I stuck my tongue out at him and he did too. We headed out.

Another job. I liked being a detective. It sure beat living on the run, hiding out in crappy motels while fearing that every knock on the door was the police—or prison. If my older brother hadn't been the first sasquatch sheriff of Nugget County, I'd be living with cement under my feet in the state pen.

But the PI job wasn't easy. Especially if you're over six feet tall and covered in beautiful brown fur. I've found a niche, though, and gotten a few cases under my belt. Yeah—it's never easy. But it's never boring either. Still, I could do with a case that was boring, easy, and paid big time.

I whispered a prayer to the Holy Woods that this one would be different, but the trees had long since gotten into the habit of ignoring me.

Harold said this Walter Rose guy was pure fancy-pants. Cloth napkins, name brand clothing, juiciest strawberry in the bush kind of fancy. Milo had gotten a constellation of ketchup stains on his polo shirt, and my checkered flannel shirt—call it a lumberjack shirt and I'll tear your arms off—could use a wash, but time was a-wasting. If this Rose dude wanted a bigfoot detective, he could put up with some bad bigfoot grooming.

We cruised out of Sarsaparilla Springs, cut over the freeway and headed south. Rolled into Terroir Valley, right on the edge of Nugget County. This was the exclusive part of Nugget County. Private schools, expensive boutiques with elegant mannequins behind wall-length windows, and trendy restaurants with unpronounceable names. My old pick-up didn't mix well with the Italian sports vehicles and luxury town cars cruising on the spotless streets. I was probably the only bigfoot around. If they caught me here overnight, they'd shave me—or put ribbons in my fur.

I followed the GPS instructions to the address Harold had given me. Out of the business area and into the surrounding fields. Wine country. Seas of trellises loaded with vines, split with the occasional shed or warehouse or tree tinged with autumn gold. The road curved into one vineyard. We went up a little hill, from pavement to fancy cobblestone, and then a set of wrought-iron gates before a low-slung mansion that looked like it could gobble up my little condo about a thousand times and still have plenty of room for dessert.

The gates creaked open, revealing a giant driveway bordered with carefully tamed vegetation and a trickling fountain. I parked.

A snooty-looking dude in a spotless navy-blue suit waited for us. Milo and I hopped out and I gave him my best bigfoot smile. "Hey there. I'm Arlo Patches, this is my nephew, Milo. It's Bring Your Cub to Work Day, I guess."

"Pleased to meet you," Milo said.

Mr. Snooty's nose wrinkled, just a little. He had no hair to speak of and brilliantly pink skin—reminded me of a coyote with mange. "My name is Thompkins. I'm Mr. Rose's assistant. If you'll follow me, please—" A gentle wave of his hand to a stone staircase jutting off the bottom of the mansion like a big root. We followed him down. "Mr. Rose is currently watching his daughter's riding lesson."

"What's she riding?" I asked.

"A thoroughbred bay mare. Old English stock." He looked at me in credulous annoyance—probably thinking I was just out of the woods and still figuring out how the human world worked.

"That's a type of horse, right?" I batted my eyes at him as we reached the bottom of the staircase.

The winery stretched into the distance, next to a big corral—rough dust and a circle of tall fence—near a neat set of stables. Animal scent, rich and redolent of horse sweat and dung, clung to everything.

A girl—maybe two or three years older than Milo—sat low in the saddle of a bay, riding the horse in an easy circle. A young woman in a barn coat and cowboy hat stood by the fence, offering encouragement. Watching both, seated at a picnic table with his feet on the bench and his behind on the tabletop, was Walter Rose himself. You could tell by the way Thompkins approached him—like a priest approaching an altar. He said something quietly to his employer.

Then Rose beckoned Milo and me closer, with a big smile. "Arlo! So glad you could come by." He had fading, graying hair above a fleshy, handsome face. "That'll be all Mr. Thompkins." His clerk nodded curtly and departed. "Apologies—he's set in his ways." I ambled over. "This is your nephew, Milo?" He grinned at the cub. "Would you like to watch Maris ride?"

Milo shrugged but headed over to the fence. More horses watched from their stalls, eyes gleaming, occasionally letting out a whicker and shaking their manes. A goat, absurdly chubby, waddled by the stable and gave me a look of pure hate.

Rose settled back—an overgrown kid in his sports coat and no-tie collared shirt. Watching his daughter make another circle. "My pride and joy."

Maris Rose had teeth like a beaver's, tamed by braces, and her reddish hair streamed behind her like flame.

"Handles that horse well," I said—not sure what else to say. I didn't know much about horses. You didn't have many of them in the California forests.

"She loves horses. Loves all animals." He flicked out his cell phone, went to a picture from some official website. A bespectacled woman in a North Face jacket and beanie, standing on some misty promontory. "Loves wolves. Which brings me to why I asked you out here. You see, a month ago, this woman from UC Davis gave a presentation for Maris's class at her school. Professor Josie Braithwaite. She studies wolves."

Wolves. A shiver crackled electric under my fur. Like what Milo had mentioned.

"You ever see any of those, out in the wilderness?" Rose asked. "Not here, but in your travels."

"No—there used to be wolves in California, way back in the day of my parents' parents, but you killed them all." I grunted—correcting myself. I had to be on best behavior. "Americans, I mean. Not you, personally. You shot them, poisoned them. Same as the Grizzly Bears. They were long gone by the time I came around. But one time…" I looked into the distance. Staring at the large autumn sun burning amongst the wisps of fall cloud. "One time we went north. Gathering of the bands. Went into what you would call Oregon. Cold and rainy up there, but one night—I could hear them. Howling through the wilderness. Thought it was ghosts. Spirits. Something not of this world."

He listened to my story. "Wow." Then smiled. "This is Dr. Braithwaite, she fell under the same spell, I suppose. Maris got hooked too. They've been corresponding—Maris wants to study wolves, you know. Dr. Braithwaite was real helpful. Responded to her emails, sent her pictures. Just really, really nice. They had an inspiring connection."

I'm sure the fact that Maris's dad had more money than the forest had pine needles didn't hurt. But I didn't say that.

I watched her make another lap. Milo watched too, as the irate goat trotted over and gave him a wary sniff. He offered the goat a tentative pet, which was—grudgingly—received.

"So, then, Dr. Braithwaite says she's coming to Nugget County. Big breakthrough, huge discovery in the Charles E. Boles State Forest. Something like that. Made Maris's day, I tell you. But, then, all of a sudden, nothing. Dr. Braithwaite just disappeared." He looked down at his loafers. "I take it that's not unusual. Or at least, that's what the people at her college said. She's doing field work. Out of cell service. That kind of thing. The police said about the same."

Field work. Didn't sound like Dr. Braithwaite was missing. Sounded like she was sleeping in a tent and pissing in the dirt. Rose was acting like a typical human. You take one step off the prescribed forest trail, and you're lost to the world.

I forced my voice gentle. "If she's doing field work—"

"I know, I know. But she's been so good about replying to Maris. Never let an email get more than a day old before responding. And she hasn't checked in for about three weeks. That, I know, is not usual. It's like she got swallowed up by the redwood jungle." Rose looked at me, voice hopeful. "You know the State Forest, right?"

Born and raised. I knew the trails around campsites particularly well, because that was where I'd swipe candy bars, bags of Cheetos, and other goodies. "Absolutely."

"Well, see if you can find her—her campsite or whatever. I don't know where it is, or even if she's still there." He snapped his fingers—playing amateur detective himself, but it was still a decent idea. "Maybe you could check with some of her friends in town. I know she had a few. Said she was staying with them before going out into the woods. Environmentalist, tree-hugger types."

Sarsaparilla Springs' Crunchy Contingent. I knew some of them too.

He nodded to Thompkins, who presented me with an envelope. Inside was a check, and marked on that check was a very nice number.

Rose didn't watch as my eyes went full moon big. He was watching his daughter. I looked up to see the love in his eyes. He'd do anything for her, and with his fortune, he could afford to. "Think you can manage that, Arlo?"

"I think so." I'd already shoved the check into my wallet.

"Wonderful." Rose hopped from the table. "How's our girl doing there, Ms. Blake?"

The riding instructor fanned her freckled face with her cowboy hat as Maris slowed her horse to a trot. "Needs some practice, I suppose—but her form's good." The bay approached, bowing her head and jabbing it at Milo, who had perched his feet on the lower rung of the fence. A whicker and a snort that made the cub's fur dance. Milo smiled back. "Looks like Caramel doesn't mind this guy around either."

Maris watched me from the saddle, reins held tight. "Honey, this is the guy who's going to find Dr. Josie," Rose said.

"You will?" Maris asked. "You'll make sure she's safe?"

I smiled. "I'll do my best."

"Please do—she's just a really, really nice person." She reached over, petting the horse. "It's cool, you know. You being a sasquatch."

"Oh yeah?" I asked.

"Sasquatches don't have to pretend to be like everyone else."

Insightful. I shrugged. "You'd be surprised." Then I waved to Milo. "Come on, furball. Time we get back to Sarsaparilla Springs, your mom will be there. Then I'll start working on the case."

"I'll send over all the details I have," Rose said. "And thank you."

"Appreciate it." I beckoned to Milo, and he scrambled over, his feet padding on the dust.

We made for the stairs with dust and bits of straw clinging to our feet—when that goat trotted into our path. It spun about and looked at me. Pure hate in those luminous eyes. Didn't know why. Sometimes, domestic critters didn't care for the Children of the Earth. We were too wild maybe. Or a nasty reminder of what they'd lost.

In any case, he lowered his head, let out a disturbingly human scream, and started galloping for me.

I grunted, flashed my shoulders—moved in front of Milo. Instinct clicking in. This goat only came up to my knee. Those horns didn't look so friendly, but I could punt the goat without much of a problem. Of course, sending the beloved pet goat of my new employer flying might send the wrong message.

Then Milo let out a call. A warbling, clear-voiced noise, far from his usual squeak. Some mix between birdsong and the gentle rush of wind through the forest. It put a chill under my fur and my toes clenched up on the stone steps.

The goat slowed his pace. Hoisted up his head—not showing me the horns. He went from a charge to a happy skip and cantered around me. Reached Milo—but I knew he was no threat.

What in the Holy Woods' name had happened?

"Hey there." Milo smoothed his hand over the goat's head like he was at a petting zoo.

"Everything okay?" Rose called out. "Apologies, Arlo—Milk Dud's got a temper."

Milo was scratching Milk Dud's chin now. "It's all good," I called back. I patted his shoulder. “Come on, furball.”

He looked at me—just as confused.

Old stories were trickling back from my memory. Old myths. If the wolves were coming back, what else could return from the world of legend?

When we got back to Sarsaparilla Springs, evening had crept in with autumnal speed. Sunset added new shades of gold to the fall leaves clustered in the big maple planted in the front yard of the Patches’ suburban house. A tame tree. Made me think of the wolves, running free in the forests so far from here—or maybe not so far, if what Dr. Braithwaite said was true. From what I understood, you couldn’t put them in the front yard. Or take them to McDonalds, give them fast food. They were wild.

Unlike me.

Rosemary Patches, my sister-in-law, was hard at work in the front yard. She looked up from setting a cardboard tombstone, painted dark gray, into the lawn, and hooted happily as Milo hurried into her arms. Her fur, a lighter buttercream, rested under a festive fall sweater embroidered with pumpkins. I walked over and we exchanged sniffs as I looked at the label on her grave.

“A dead human is under here.” I hummed. “Rosemary—is there something I don’t know?”

“Halloween decoration, silly. I’ve been studying North American fall traditions for a long time and decided to take part. They love this kind of stuff—covering their homes in macabre decorations. Sometimes, decorative tombstones have some sort of clever message on them, but I figured that it was best to be direct.”

“Mom?” Milo pointed to another decoration—the skeleton of a t-rex perched by the door. “Is that really Halloween-y?”

“Skeletons are a common human symbol for Halloween, Milo.”

Rosemary taught anthropology at Nugget County Junior College. Her class was always in high demand, because of her unique perspective. I walked to the dino skeleton and rested my hand amongst the plastic teeth. “Maybe give it a witch’s hat or something.”

“Great idea,” Rosemary agreed. “Heard from Harold—he’ll be here a bit later. Would you like to join us for dinner?”

I considered it. Rosemary would serve a massive bowl of salad, wild grasses and herbs sprinkled with generous amounts of bark and berries. A traditional bigfoot banquet. I’d probably drench mine in salad dressing, and she’d be nice enough to pretend not to notice.

But that check had settled in my pocket like a weight and the dream of wolves clung to me like a bur. I wanted to get started.

"Gotta take a rain check, Rosemary. Appreciate it."

"But you'll be there for Halloween, right?" Milo asked from the doorway.

"Absolutely, furball. What are you gonna be?"

"I'm keeping my options open." He spoke with pure preciousness. "Between Luke Skywalker and Mario."

"What are you gonna be, Arlo?"

I grunted. "Bigfoot."

"Real clever." Rosemary started for the door, arm around her son.

Should I tell her about his voice? How a call from him had stopped a goat in its tracks? Maybe things like this had happened before—maybe she'd understand. Or maybe she'd be upset. They were already heading into the comfort of their house. I kept my mouth closed. Something Rose's daughter, Maris, said came back to me. Sasquatches didn't have to pretend to be like everyone else. Well, maybe they didn't *have* to—but I wanted normality for Milo.

I knew his parents did too.

They headed inside and I went back to my pick-up.

I cruised out of the suburban sprawl leaking from the side of Sarsaparilla Springs and into the town proper. Some signs of night life—orange lights gleaming outside the newly-opened craft brewery by the Darling Clementine Bed and Breakfast, a good crowd at the Fat Fox Diner—but it was a Wednesday, and the tourists wouldn't be coming in big time until the weekend. I imagined there'd be quite a few as we got closer to Halloween. Humans in crazy costumes, boozing hard, causing mayhem as they partied their way up and down the blocks.

Using every excuse they could to act animal.

At the far end of the main drag, I parked outside an egg-shaped building with a life-sized statue of bigfoot out front—one of those massive wooden hulks sculpted with a chainsaw. Not a bad likeness, but his teeth were clenched, and his eyes bulged a little too big.

Looked constipated.

I headed into The Nugget County Sasquatch Society's Bigfoot Museum.

I'd always enjoyed Squatch Hunters, like the sort who made this museum back in the day. A bunch of well-meaning, foolish humans, crashing around the forest, making ridiculous fake hoots and spraying supposedly authentic bigfoot musk everywhere. Me and some of the other bad cubs in the band would delight in pranking them—leaving just enough hair on the trail or

I CRUISED OUT OF THE URBAN SPRAWL...

tantalizing them with hoots to lead them on, then doubling back and hiding our laughter as they stumbled around like blind moles. Harold found them annoying, and thought it was mean to lead them on.

But, say what you will about them, they liked the Children of the Earth—when we left the woods, they became some of our biggest supporters. That was more than you could say for a lot of humans.

The door of the Bigfoot Museum was unlocked, but the place was empty. Statues, exhibits, trays of artifacts, a few videos silently playing. "Sebastian?" I called for the owner. "You in there?" You'd think that big sasquatch reveal would put the place out of business, but Sebastian Kowalski had pivoted to making the place a celebration of Northern California bigfoot culture. Rosemary had consulted on the exhibits, which was how I knew him.

Still a little weird to see pictures of your band on the walls, mixed with decommissioned ritual antlers, twig toothbrushes displayed like they were arcane artifacts. He'd even asked to use me as a model for a plaster display of authentic bigfoot prints. Weird, I know—but he paid generously.

"Over here, man!" Kowalski called from the side room. I walked in and found him bopping to pop music as he looked over mannequins of different Children varieties. A pale-furred yeti, a dark Russian alma, a Chinese yeren with its coat of gold. The song was 'Abominable'—Taylor Swift's latest collab with Shambhala Sam, the yeti pop star. Kowalski fumbled with his phone to switch it off. "Sorry, my dude. I usually stick to the Stones and the Dead, but I couldn't resist the first breakout Children star, you know?"

"I heard the Kidz Bop version when I drove Milo's carpool." I looked at the assorted mannequins. Their fur had been made of felt and their plastic fangs shone in the light. "You want to make one that looks like me?"

"Oh, dude—that'd be awesome." Kowalski had a salt-and-pepper beard and a salt-and-pepper mane, glasses with big plastic frames, and an easy smile. Maybe the I Heart Bigfoot t-shirt was a little much, but I couldn't help liking the guy. "You know, I was considering having something about your family. Your big brother's the first sasquatch sheriff, ever. Your sister's been on the news like tons of times for her advocacy, and, you, ah—"

He faltered and I didn't blame him. What was he gonna say? While Harold and Harriet soared, I was everything wrong with the attempt of bigfeet to join the world of man. Dropping out of community college, running with a bad crowd—sliding into petty crime and then big-time bank robbery.

And now I was a low-rent PI, circling the drain.

"It's all good." I offered him a smile. "Actually, Sebastian, I'm here about a case. Someone you might know."

"Oh yeah?" He motioned to the cushioned bench facing a screening of the

Patterson Film—jury was still out if that was a prankster in a costume or one of the Children going for a morning walk. Our band's elders had tried to find the culprit, but no one fessed up. "Do tell."

Rose had texted me some more information. I showed him the picture of Dr. Josie Braithwaite. "She ever come here?"

His face lit up. "Dr. Josie! Yeah!" I knew it. Crunchy types tended to congregate—birds of a feather. "She visited the museum and we hit it off, been corresponding. Wolves in the woods, man. Now that there's no question that squatches are out there, wolves are the next big thing. In this part of California, they're the new cryptozoology. Besides aliens, of course."

"There's no such thing as aliens," I said. "Are there?"

He arched his shaggy eyebrows.

"Let's stick with the wolves. Dr. Braithwaite thought some had come down here?"

"A big pack of Northern Rocky Mountain Wolves crossed the border from Oregon and settled here. Got reintroduced to the Yellowstone, Canada, and now they're coming back to the places their ancestors used to run, way back in the day." He folded his legs. "Dr. Josie told me all these benefits. They'll keep the deer population in check, make sure the vegetation grows right. Take out sick animals too, so the prey animals get healthier. They're a keystone species, you know—of course you do. Charismatic Megafauna—that's the term she used."

"I'm kind of a Charismatic Megafauna myself."

He paused. "But not everyone likes wolves."

"No?"

"Well, they did kill them all for a reason, you know. Fear of attack—even though you're more likely to get struck by lightning than lunched by a wolf. But they prey on farm animals. Sheep, goats, cattle. A wolf snacks on part of a commercial herd, that's like a couple hundred bucks down the drain. And you can't actually kill them. They're federally protected. If wolves are creeping around Nugget County, then where they are becomes protected habitat, even beyond what's in the park. Farmers know that. Dr. Josie mentioned that she was worried about anyone finding the wolves before her and practicing the three S's."

"What are those?"

"Shoot Them, Shovel Them, Shut Up."

Holy Woods.

I thought back to the parking lot and my little tactical tomahawk showdown. "Like the Jefferson Rangers."

"I don't know about that. Some of them are good guys. I get my goat and sheep cheese from Candlewick Ranch at the Farmer's Market. That stuff rules." But he scrunched up his lips, fidgeted on his seat. The fear tang crept off him, an acrid scent mixing with the gentle air conditioning of the museum.

"Was Dr. Josie worried? About the Rangers, or anyone else?"

He looked at me, and I could tell the friendly conversation was coming to an end.

"I'm trying to find her, Sebastian. That's what I've been hired to do. I want to make sure she's all right—her and the wolves." I settled next to him. Reinforced bench—it only creaked a little at my weight. "I've helped you with the museum—I'll help you some more. Tell you some of the Children's myths and folktales, if that helps. Perfect for Halloween."

"Quid pro quo, Arlo?"

"What's that mean?"

"You do something for me, I do something for you—is that it?"

I grunted. "Look, man—I'm on your side. I'm on Dr. Josie's side."

"And what side is that?"

"The wilderness."

He listened carefully and pushed his glasses back up the bridge of his nose. Closed his eyes and opened them. "We were in touch during her field work in the woods. She'd visit the museum when she came into town; ask me for advice on trails, camping spots—and places wolves might want to go. I know the State Forest pretty well. Spent a lot of time looking for you guys, after all. I gave her advice, told her to go near the border of the Snake River Indian Reservation. But this week, she didn't show up. And before that, she was worried."

Sometimes, the best thing a detective can do is stay quiet. Mountain lions have learned that lesson well.

"First off, when she saw me last, she said she was being followed. Wasn't sure, of course. But the pair following her—I guess they kind of stood out." He scratched the back of his neck. "They were like you, but a different subspecies. Big feathery tails. Black fur with white stripes. And the smell—she said they stank. From what I've read, I'd say they were South Florida Skunk Apes."

Skunk apes. Oh boy.

"Their clothing—was it kind of flashy? Gold chains, designer clothing, that sort of thing."

He bobbed his head. "Yeah. That's what she said. You know them?"

"Did the male have a mullet?"

"Yup."

I groaned. A deep, sad rumble coming from the bottom of my belly. "I know them."

"So, should I be worried? About Dr. Josie?"

"Not from them." But I didn't say that fear was the wrong choice. "She say anything else?"

"No—but then, just yesterday, she sent me a picture." He had a laptop perched on the display case showing off some Tibetan artifacts and photos from the Dalai Lama's first press conference with yeti leaders. He snapped it open. "I—I don't know what to do with it." He snapped open the computer and flicked it on the screen. We gathered around like cubs examining an interesting bug.

There on the screen, a nighttime photo. Dark pavement, thick Redwood Forest behind. Glowing bright with the flash of a camera. A Nugget County road sign, showing directions for Sarsaparilla Springs, the Snake River Reservation.

Right below the sign, a wolf.

No mistaking it. No doubt that this was a wolf and not a big coyote. The size, the power beneath that gray fur, told you everything. The wolf looked surprised, its eyes reflecting the glow of the camera flash like it had silver fire in the sockets. Pure wildness in that poise, ears tented, muscles tense, ready to run for the underbrush in a moment's notice.

You couldn't look at that and imagine it ever being tamed.

Kowalski pointed to the wolf. "That's dynamite, man. I put that out in the world, there's no telling what'll happen." He closed the computer screen. "Environmental laws. Reactionaries rising against them. Nugget County gets set on fire, and I don't know if that's what Dr. Josie would want." He leaned back. "I respect your opinion, Arlo. What do you think I should do?"

Those Jefferson Rangers in the parking lot, so sure that they were the masters of this world. Walter Rose and his daughter, pleading for another way. Milo—calling off that goat. Using an ancient power, something that I had thought was a myth.

A promise that the Children of the Earth had made to all living things.

We had to keep that promise.

I patted the computer. "That's dynamite?"

"Yeah."

I hooted. A powerful, panting bigfoot noise that echoed through the quiet museum. "Set it off."

He grinned and let out a chuckle, which I shared.

Like it or not, the wilderness was coming back.

I made it back to my duplex late. Fumbled with the key and went inside—nearly tripping over my cat. Patterson—I'd named him after the film—weaved around my legs in a chubby tabby swirl, meowing piteously. I picked him up, tucked him under my arm, and looked inside. A little metropolis of garbage coated my coffee table and the couch. Fast food bags, pizza boxes, Chinese food cartons, with a healthy sprinkling of beer bottles. I carried Patterson over the mess to the counter, where stacks of Fancy Feast waited. He squirmed in delight as I fumbled with the can opener.

Why'd they make these things so small?

The pink cylinder of cat food splatted into his dish. Patterson attacked it. I watched him devour the grub happily. If you were domestic, you expected your food to be delivered to you. Of course, I was no different. I did my foraging in supermarkets and drive-thrus now.

"Good stuff, buddy?" I asked, popping the fridge. I grabbed a mass of veggie burritos, tossed them in the microwave, and selected a pair of beers while I waited. My nightly routine. Often enough, the guy in the adjacent duplex, dude named Ramon, would have me over for meals and movies. His boyfriend's car was parked out front though, and he hadn't texted me, so I guess he wanted some privacy.

Oh well—that left me and Patterson.

I grabbed the grub, settled onto the couch, and switched on the television. Flipped through streaming services.

Horror movies—werewolf movies.

Man turning into a beast. The prospect fascinated humans. Judging by the number of movies with that theme, they couldn't get enough of it. Of course, from my experience, man was generally the scarier of the two. But I looked at the mess in my room, thought about how long it had been since I slept in a nest of leaves and branches—and how I didn't want to do that again—and realized something: I'd gone ahead and done a beast-to-man transformation myself.

We all had. Harold enforced human law. Rosemary taught human students. Milo had never spent a night in the woods without a tent and a sleeping bag.

Maybe that's why I wanted Kowalski to release that picture. It was spite.

I leaned back and moaned. Patterson came over and plopped into my lap. I moved my hand up and down his back and he pressed himself against me, letting out a rumbling purr. So much of my life had been done out of spite—and I don't recall it ever working out.

The next morning, I nuked a breakfast burrito, gave Patterson his meal, and fired up my computer—an extra-large model Rosemary had gotten me last Christmas to practice American gift-giving traditions. Dr. Braithwaite's unwanted stinky followers were a pair of skunk ape outlaws named Stinko and Daisy. Wasn't entirely sure that it was them—there were plenty of skunk apes in the world, most hanging around their home in the Everglades—but I'd shave myself naked if they weren't the culprits. Easy enough to find out. Two skunk apes dressed like hypebeast royalty and strutting around Northern California would be simple enough to find, but this pair made it even easier—they left their own slime trail of social media posts.

I swung over to their website—Stenchlife.com—and scrolled through info set amongst eye-searing neon blobs and splotches. Stinko and Daisy were more than just Skunk Ape Bonnie and Clyde: Stinko was an aspiring DJ and social media influencer. He had a music video at the center—Money Swamp—and I gave it a watch. Stinko bouncing around on a fanboat while the camera zoomed in and out wildly, the wind in his wild mullet, and shots of him trying to crown an irate gator with his trucker hat. I'd had better times after rolling around in poison oak.

A notification blinked in his updates. I was in luck—he was starting a brand new livestream. I switched to his feed.

"What up, Stink Fam? Stinko here." Stinko appeared, seated at a table in a restaurant—Sarsaparilla Springs' main street gleaming with fall dawn right behind him. "You know that I'm a skunk ape with appetite, so check out my order here at the Fat Fox Diner." He spun the camera around to show his plate. "I'm talking pancake short stack—strawberries inside, of course—English muffin with three fried eggs, veggie bacon, veggie sausage, veggie Canadian bacon, and French toast." He shoved a bottle of hot sauce into the camera. "And you know how it is—if it ain't spicy, it ain't stinking!" He worked the bottle, dousing everything with bright orange drops.

I caught a glimpse of Daisy sitting across from him, oversized Gucci shades drooping to reveal tired, shiny dark eyes.

Fat Fox Diner was downtown. If I booked it, I could be there in time to catch them paying the check.

Patterson brushed against my leg. Did he want seconds? He was gonna have to wait. "Sorry, big guy." I hastened to the closet. "It's hunting season."

I put on a Western shirt and a golf jacket—Big and Tall bargain bin purchases—then got to my car. Brought the pick-up to downtown Sarsaparilla Springs and the Fat Fox Diner. The place was an institution—classic diner food, huge menus, and they even had a good selection of veggie items for bigfoots. I passed the wooden statue of a plump fox outside and headed in. Took a seat at the chrome spaceship counter, ordered a coffee, and checked the mirror behind the bar.

Stinko and Daisy sat in a booth by the window, their livestream apparently finished. A few other patrons occupied the restaurant, though we were past the breakfast rush and not quite at lunch. I put on a Giants cap for a quick disguise, positioned myself a little closer to Stinko and Daisy, and hunched over my coffee. Had they clocked me? We'd had a few run-ins before—a botched casino heist out west. But no—both were lost in their phones, Stinko busying himself with a napkin, trying to scrape stains from his silk shirt.

"Oh man—this is Versace!" Stinko's feathery brushtail drooped. "When are we supposed to meet with Wambach?"

Daisy checked something on her phone. "Around lunchtime." Neither bothered whispering.

"Think we got time to go to a laundromat or something? Or maybe we can break into a house—use their washer and dryer?"

"You want to add a B and E to our jacket, hon?" Daisy showed her teeth. "Besides, I don't want to be late. That Wambach guy—I'll be honest, babe—he scares the hell out of me."

"Ah, he's not so bad." Stinko leaned across the table, giving her a nuzzle. "Just thinks he's the biggest gator in the swamp, is all."

Wambach. Not a name I knew. Was he who had hired Stinko and Daisy to follow Dr. Braithwaite? Something told me they didn't do it on their own so they could corner her for intense academic discussions.

"We'll head over there after—" He fell silent and pointed to the TV mounted above the counter. "Damn. That's one big dog."

I craned my head for a look. Everyone in the diner did. The TV showed news—national news. And there was the picture from Sebastian Kowalski's computer, originally taken by Dr. Braithwaite. The sign. The wolf at night. The glow of those eyes.

Captioned words at the bottom revealed the anchor's dialogue. "Biologists have confirmed that this is a wolf and may be a part of a theorized pack currently living in Northern California. Wolves are protected by the Endangered Species Act and—"

A rustle in the back of the restaurant. I swiveled. It was Ollie Candle and his fellow Ranger, Jerome. None of them had their militia costumes on now—just jeans and windbreakers. Both watched the screen with eyes that matched those of the wolf. Wide, watchful, careful.

Hunter's eyes.

They started out, Candle swinging by the counter to settle his bill. As he got his card back, he glanced at me. I stared back. Was he still raw about what had happened in the elementary school parking lot yesterday? No fear in his scent. Just determination.

He turned and walked out.

I'd asked Kowalski to release the wolf pic out of spite—anger at myself, maybe. If I'd given up the wild, maybe it didn't matter because something else hadn't.

But what had I unleashed instead?

SKUNK APE SHENANIGANS

I forced my eyes from the TV. Back to the mirror—just in time to see Stinko and Daisy getting up to leave. They went for the door as I finished my coffee, Stinko pointing up ahead and letting out a squeal of joy. "Oh man—Daisy, check this out!" He motioned across the street to Woodland Memories, a kitschy tourist shop specializing in t-shirts with dumb slogans and stuffed animals. Locals would sooner smooch a porcupine's backside than go in there. "Come on, babe—we gotta go!" He all but dragged her across the street.

Worth keeping up the tail? Definitely. I knew they were supposed to meet a dude named Wambach, knew they feared him, but that was about it. Nothing about Dr. Josie. Nothing about who hired them.

I finished my coffee, paid, and hit the street.

A few dead leaves, spectacular fall colors, had settled on the sidewalk. Stinko and Daisy jaywalked—getting a honk from a passing SUV—and went into Woodland Memories. Easy to make out their forms behind the glass, Stinko's mullet-topped profile, numerous necklaces and medallions shimmering bright. I slipped across as well.

They'd gone into the back of the store, and I stayed in the front. Snagged a guide to hiking trails and flipped through it while occasionally looking at them. A small crowd—all tourists in LL Bean finery—wandered amongst the displays, purchasing sunscreen and stuffed squirrels. Besides the Skunk Ape Power Couple, I was the only Child there, so I played it sneaky and stuck to the shadows.

"Hey—hey, Daisy." Stinko grabbed one of the biggest stuffed bears that I'd ever seen. An enormously obese teddy bear—more of a beanbag chair than a stuffy. It had a black bear's dark fur and button nose. "What do you think of my new friend? I'm gonna buy him."

"Are you serious?" Daisy asked. "Where we gonna put that?"

"Convertible's big enough. He can ride behind you." He plopped the huge bear in her hands.

Awesome—they were shopping. How long until they started talking business again?

But I should've known better. For Stinko and Daisy, the journey always beat the destination. They'd been swimming around in swamps for most of their lives, dodging gator jaws and mosquitos, and were now loose in the human world with all its joys. The Harrowers had a whole lot of pleasure for the taking. I knew that better than most—and I almost envied the skunk apes their joie de vivre.

If only they didn't keep doing illegal activities to fund it.

"Oh—Daisy—Look—we gotta get this one for the feed!" Stinko had moved to the side of the store, where a big wooden cut-out photo-op waited. It was pure cheese: a dopey ranger chasing after a sasquatch holding a picnic basket. A Yogi Bear rip-off, with holes for the ranger and squatch's face, so tourists could poke their faces through. "You want to be the ranger or the bigfoot?"

Daisy trotted over to join him, still carrying the massive stuffed bear. "Do we have to?"

"Come on, it'll be fun—then we'll get back to the search. Maybe check that museum we passed on the way in here. Scientists like museums, don't they?" So they definitely were searching for Dr. Braithwaite—and hadn't found her. "But we both gotta be in the post for it to really do numbers. Let me see if I can find someone who'd be willing to..."

His head swiveled. I didn't duck in time.

Stinko let out a hoot of pure, unadulterated joy. "Arlo! Arlo Patches!"

Oh no.

It was bad luck. No—it was the work of the Holy Trees. When you climbed high, they enjoyed breaking the branches below you.

I forced myself to look up from the guidebook. "Yeah?"

"Arlo—it's me, Stinko!" If he hadn't been scanning the place, if he hadn't chosen to take a stupid picture, I'd have been golden. But he did, so I wasn't. "Arlo, get over here." He waved me over, beaming. "You remember me and Daisy, right? From that casino thing?"

I joined them. "How could I forget?"

"Oh man—talk about some wild times." Stinko laughed, showing his fangs. "Look, bro, I hope I didn't give you much trouble. Kind of left you holding the bag. But if it makes you feel any better, Daisy and I didn't hold onto that cash for long. We hit Stockton, got involved with some Russians—it was a mess." He shook his head fondly. "How you been, Arlo? You been good?"

"I've been busy," I said.

"Still in the detective business?" Daisy flicked her tail back and forth.

I shrugged. "What can I say? Beats unemployment." Did she suspect? Daisy was certainly the brains of the operation, and her eyes shone, her mouth open—tongue resting on the point of one of her fangs. Thinking things through. "Look, I'd love to catch up—but I'm actually on a case now—"

"Oh, we won't keep you." Stinko shoved his phone into my hand and darted back. "Okay, Daisy—I'll be the ranger, you be the squatch trying to get away. How's that sound?"

But Daisy didn't move. Even as I gripped the phone, flipping it around to fix the camera on the cut-out, she didn't do her part and get into position. Instead, she pointed at me. "You like the Fat Fox Diner, Arlo?"

I stared straight back. "Best breakfast potatoes in town."

"Daisy, what are you doing?" Stinko had already put an alarming open-mouthed smile on his face. Showed off the gold caps he'd slid over several of his teeth, a few shimmering with what looked like gemstones. "Come on—I can't hold like this forever."

Then Daisy's inquisitive look faded. The other big foot dropped. "You've been following us, honey."

What was I gonna do? Deny it? Say that getting a coffee and going into Woodland Memories was my morning routine? That would fly about as well as a marmot. I held up my hands instead, letting out a little whimper. Putting on my best 'I'm sorry I didn't do my homework' expression that I'd learned from Milo. "Daisy, Stinko—I think you guys are in trouble. You don't know what you're—"

Daisy spun the huge stuffed bear around and smashed it into my face.

Taking a wallop in a pillow fight isn't enough to do any real damage—but a pillow wielded with all the muscle of a skunk ape is a different story. The giant stuffed animal bear gave me a massive kiss, the thwack wrapping my face in fluff and fuzz. Didn't knock me down—but it sent me stumbling back—my feet slipping on the polished floor of Woodland Memories. I bumped into a display of water bottles, my shoulder slipping against a shelf. The water bottles—the heavy, hulking metal sorts—rained down and did a little dance on my head and back.

I glared up at Daisy as she lowered the stuffed bear. "That—" A final water bottle descended and banged off my skull. I clenched my teeth. "You didn't have to do that."

She grabbed the edge of the squatch and ranger photo op and tugged it down—sending it crashing into my face. My head wedged into the hole for the sasquatch, the cheap wood scratching my neck. Then she grabbed Stinko by the arm and started dashing for the door, rushing past the surprised tourists who looked on in horror at the bigfoot brawl.

I grabbed the edges of the sign and pushed. It dragged against my chin. Scraped my ears. An adjustment of the head and the damn thing was off—and then I sprang up, grunting and bruised and not in a mood to be nice. I started for the door, chasing after the designer jackets of the skunk apes as they made it to the door. Daisy had it open, the little bell giving its merry ring, as I pounded after them with all the grace of a chunky bear loping toward prey.

Stinko paused and looked over his shoulder. "Arlo, man." He tugged at his Versaci belt, lowering his pants as he gripped the door for support. "I thought you were cool."

Then he flashed his bottom at me. A sort of nasty pimple right where the sun don't shine flexed and erupted—giving me a second to duck a massive volley of greenish-yellow gunk hurtling through the air in a shimmering cascade.

I caught part of the volley. It splashed my shirt and golf jacket and jeans—even got in my face.

The smell—a sort of extremely potent, sense-shriveling, rotten, far-too garlicky blast—burned into my nostrils.

I tumbled back, smashed into another display. More stuffed animals. They avalanched all over me as the stink hammered my nose and the breakfast burrito threatened to crawl up my throat and come flying out to join the fun.

I blinked. Sputtered. Coughed and gagged. Finally opened my eyes.

A stuffed wolf had fallen from the display and settled on my belly. It stared at me with placid plastic eyes.

Great.

I sat up as a few tourist types and a terrified teenaged clerk with one of them fuzzy Russian hats came around to stare at me. I picked up the stuffed animal and stood. My little audience covered their noses—skunk ape stink lingered. It stuck around like a wound. Worse than that, Daisy and Stinko were gone. They might be dumb, but they weren't that dumb. They'd motor out of here and keep a lookout for me. Any plans of tailing them were as ruined as my shirt.

"Uh—sorry about that." I fumbled for my wallet. "I'll cover the damages." More accurately, Walter Rose would. Hopefully, I could bill this little episode to the hefty expense account he'd given me—I'd just switch it around a little, describe it in a way that was less embarrassing. The worst damage would be to my pride.

Then something else caught my eye.

A little square, shimmering and green, on the floor. I picked it up.

Gator-skin pattern on the case. Big picture of a frog hoisting up twin middle fingers on the lock screen. No doubt about it—this was Stinko's phone.

I pocketed it.

Maybe the Holy Woods were looking out for me after all.

I settled the bill with Woodland Memories and drove home, setting down some old towels on my car seats to make sure none of the skunk ape stench dripped there. The gunk had solidified by now—something like dried snot mixed with ancient mayonnaise, but even more disgusting. I nearly retched during the little drive back to my condo. Patterson came pawing over for his usual greeting, took one sniff at me, and dashed for the kitchen like a ginger torpedo. I knew how he felt.

A shower was next. Back in the forest, there was no real solution for skunk spray. You could groom yourself for hours, dive in a mudhole and bake in the sun, or sit in a stream for days—and the stench would still stick. But humans, as with so much else, had attacked the problem with scientific intensity. I was happy to use their discovery.

Peroxide from my first aid kit. Baking soda and dish soap from my kitchen. I mixed them up, drenched myself in it, and sat in the shower while Merle Haggard sang about how his mama tried to raise him right—and failed.

My mother was still in the forest. If she could see me now, she'd probably dunk me in a pine-scented mud pit and put me on acorn-collecting duty for a month. Let that be a lesson to Porcupine not to stick his nose where it didn't belong.

Sorry, mama—that's my job now.

After the shower and a beyond thorough deodorant session, I did the self-smell test as I headed to the kitchen. The scent was nose-wrinkling bad, not puke-nonstop awful. An improvement. Thank the Sacred Trees for human ingenuity.

I settled in the kitchen, hauled out an extra-large pack of Super Spicy Cheetos for brain food, and plugged Stinko's phone into one of my chargers as I looked it over. That frog looked back at me, still flashing his middle-fingered salute. I smiled at him, shoved a fistful of Cheetos into my mouth, and examined the number pad.

Password time. I had some options. Ramon, my neighbor, worked in tech. Besides inviting me over for movie night, he was nice enough to help me with all the technical details of the human world. Could he crack a phone? I didn't know, but it was worth a shot. He'd be home that afternoon and I could swing by and check with him.

In the meantime, I could try an experiment. If I was a wannabe skunk ape influencer who put every brain cell into living large and getting into trouble, what was something simple and memorable, easy to punch in with oversized fingers, that I could set for my password?

How about 1111?

I punched it in. The phone unlocked.

"You have got to be kidding me." I set the phone down. Could almost imagine Stinko's reasoning. *It's genius, actually. The last thing anyone would expect.*

Well, Stinko, you've given me a face full of gunk, so the least you could do was make it easy for me to access your phone.

I chewed Cheetos and looked closer. First, a million social media updates came down like a snowmelt-swollen stream. Stuff praising Stinko's newest single as being 'Straight Fire,' or hateful comments saying it was 'Gator Poo.' Anything relevant to following Dr. Josie? I doubted it and swiped them all away. Could always go back and read them later if I was feeling masochistic.

Next, I swung to his Maps app and looked at previous trips. Classic detective trick. Skip tracing was easy when you had a little computer in your pocket saying where you went. Humans had done this to themselves for reasons I couldn't understand—though my phone would probably give up my location, with some coaxing. Convenience, I suppose—it always tasted good going down and you never noticed the poison kick in until it was too late.

Stinko's prior trips weren't particularly interesting as I looked through the last couple days. He'd visited fast food joints and diners—a designer clothing store in Terroir Valley. Nightclubs in San Francisco. This was Stinko's pleasure, not business.

But one address stuck out.

The Terroir Valley Country Club. He'd visited the place three times in the past week. I snapped open my laptop and went to work with the keys. The country club looked as ritzy and exclusive as you'd expect for a place in Terroir Valley. Spotless well-lit dining rooms, rolling, expansive golf course with painfully green tame grass, and smiling well-heeled clientele. Why would Stinko and Daisy go there? Sampling the buffet? Quick game of tennis?

Or were they meeting someone? Someone with the money to hire two skunk apes for a tail job?

If Stinko and Daisy were dead ends, maybe this country club would offer another lead. One way to find out.

Cheeto dust had accrued thick on my chin fuzz and hands. I went to the sink to wash them clean, gave myself another sniff. Almost presentable.

It would have to be good enough for the country club.

I went to my closet to get ready when my phone rang. A glance at the screen showed Rosemary. I answered as I stepped over an empty pizza box. "Rosemary—kind of in the middle of something."

"No worries, Arlo—just a quick check in." She sounded excited. "The wolf picture? You seen it?"

"Um—sounds familiar."

"It's big news, Arlo—huge news." She hummed. "Milo's been talking about it non-stop—same with my students." Excitement giving way to delight. "It's like the Guardian Tree. A legend becoming real. It will be like it was when the old ones were young."

Then I remembered the Jefferson Rangers leaving the Fat Fox Diner in a huff. "Not everyone's happy."

"Yeah. There's actually going to be a community meeting tonight at Milo's school, in the gym, to address concerns about the wolves. Harold's going to speak. I know he'd love to have you there." A quick pause, and the words kept spilling out. "Oh—and Harriet's heard about it too. The news is going up and down the state. All over the world. She'll be coming up tonight."

Harriet—my little sister. Treetop. So named because that's where she'd always climb.

I grunted. "Be nice to see her."

"Can you make it to the meeting?"

I opened my closet—trying to find the best outfit. "I'll try my best, Rosemary—but I'm a little busy at the moment."

I pulled into the lot a little after lunch time. Strictly high-end sports cars and luxury mom minivans lined up in the fall sunlight. My old pick-up wouldn't pass muster, so I secreted it away at the far end and walked to the main complex—a low slung expanse of white marble that looked like the capitol building of a small country. Tame trees massaged into teardrop shapes rested in planters, flanking the huge doors. I let a couple of women in designer tennis outfits, dripping in jewelry, slip past me and slid through the front door.

Massive marble lobby. Huge desk at the front, where a young woman with a polo shirt bearing the country club logo manned the desk. She had an expansive bun that made her look like she was wearing a giant walnut on the top of her head and stared at me like I'd wandered straight out of the forest and ended up here by mistake.

But I'd come prepared. I wore a trendy blazer and a t-shirt with the

Rolling Stones lip logo spilling out of a sasquatch mouth—ordered special for moments like this. I flipped off a pair of sunglasses, pocketed them, and gave Ms. Walnut Hair my biggest smile.

"Hi there, how are you doing?" I tossed a business card her way—Ramon had helped me design them. "My name's Bobby Bark. I'm a personal assistant for Shambhala Sam." The world loved that yeti pop star.

Ms. Clerk's eyes went wide as lakes. "Shambhala Sam? Oh man—that's amazing. 'How Cold Is Your Heart' is so good—that's like, that's like one of my favorite songs—and his collab with BTS—"

"Life-changing, I know." She was the perfect mark for a detective—like so many humans, she wanted to believe. I leaned closer, making my voice go conspiratorial. "Good to know you're a fan. I've got some happy news. Shambhala Sam's performing in San Francisco as part of his Mantras of Romance Tour, and he wants to spend time over here. You know—drink a little wine, take a hike, get away from it all. And he heard this place would be perfect—"

"Oh my god—it totally would be." She started throwing brochures my way. "I've got info about all our amenities, our meals, our guest program—" Maybe she'd done this before, tooting the country club's horn in case Tom Cruise or someone came to town.

"That's okay. I'm sure everything's wonderful." I put on my best bigfoot smile. "But Sam—well, he's a Child of the Earth. Like me." A yeti rather than a bigfoot, but the difference was lost on most people—we were just different flavors of the same ice cream. "And he'd like to know if other Children of the Earth have been here. If they enjoyed the amenities that this place offers."

Her spiel stopped. That was probably something Tom Cruise wasn't too concerned about.

"So, are there any Children of the Earth members?"

"Um." Ms. Walnut Head bit her lip. "No?" Like she was asking me.

I forced disappointment into my voice. "Not a single one?"

She brightened. "We've had—we've had a few, ah, Children purchase guest passes. A wonderful couple was here a few times last week. They had, ah, black fur? With a white stripe?" She was obviously uncomfortable, and I nodded to reassure her—that had to be Stinko and Daisy. "Oh—and there's Mr. Grey—he was with them. He's so charming." She pointed behind me. "We're in luck. There he is right now."

I looked over my shoulder.

Sure enough, another Child had walked in—and he certainly was the kind to be noticed. Big, even for a bigfoot—though I think he was another species. He had shoulders like mountain ranges and limbs like sequoias. Fur the color

"SO, THERE ANY CHILDREN OF THE EARTH MEMBERS?"

of mist-soaked stone—a deep gray—with eyes to match. His face, craggy and weathered, had a pair of nasty scars around his lips—curving upwards on his cheeks to grotesquely expand his natural smile. But the strangest part of it all was his clothing: a three-piece suit and plaid vest that fit him as well as his fur. Even his tie was neatly knotted.

My clothes mostly came from a Big and Tall's bargain bin—this nice outfit had to have been tailored. The store that did it probably used up all their fabric.

Mr. Grey winked one of those glittering gray eyes at the receptionist and padded down the hall. "Afternoon, love!" An accent like one of those shaggy dwarf dudes from Milo's favorite fantasy video games. Scottish, I think.

He'd noticed me—of course he had, I tended to stand out. But it didn't mean anything. I was just a particularly handsome bigfoot. "Seems promising. Could I buy a day pass? Just to have a look around?"

"Absolutely. Please let our staff know if you have any further questions." She got the paperwork ready as I pulled out my card—more expenses that Rose could deduct. "And, ah, would you mind if I ask you, kind of a personal, question?" She squinted at me—clearly nervous. "Ah—there seems to be a sort of smell around you, that some of, um, our members might find—objectionable."

The politest possible way to let me know that I stank.

I filled out the paperwork with Bobby Bark's name. "Shambhala Sam's releasing a new line of Himalayan-themed fragrances for men. Insisted that I try this one out. It's called Eau de Yak." Another smile. "I'll have to tell him it's not a winner."

"It smells, um, real natural."

I snagged the guest pass and looked down the hall. Mr. Grey had already turned the corner, but his own scent lingered. Not as bad as mine. Mountain flowers and mist. I went after him. Thankfully, Mr. Grey didn't go far.

He'd gone straight into the small restaurant occupying the veranda overlooking the golf course. Even better—the outdoors and assorted smells of the perfumed guests enjoying drinks and chicken salad sandwiches would hide my scent.

Just to make sure, I selected a seat behind a hedge dappled with particularly aromatic flowers. I pretended to look over the brochures while checking out the scene through the reflection in the polished glass of the doors.

Mr. Grey at least was easy to see. A stony mountain surrounded by pastel golf shirts and tennis dresses. More interesting was the guy he'd joined—someone else who didn't exactly fit in.

"Wambach." Mr. Grey held out his hand. "How's life treating you?"

Wambach. Stinko and Daisy had been talking about him. They seemed scared of the guy and I could see why.

Wambach was a big human. Shaved sasquatch-big. He had arms thick with jailhouse muscle, a bullet head shaved clean and tired, half-closed eyes. He'd crammed his massive body into a button-up and jeans. What you'd wear to an office—but he didn't look like the sort to spend a lot of time in a cubicle. Matter of fact, he looked like a mountain lion relaxing in the sun—all coiled, tense muscle and claws ready to slip out. I itched under my fur just looking at him.

It was fear. The kind that prey feels when the predator is on the prowl.

The big man settled back, eyes scanning the crowd. "How's life treating me? I don't know, man. Can't complain." A dry, tired voice—unburdened by much emotion.

"Ah, that's always been my attitude." Mr. Grey hooted loudly at a passing waitress. "Oi! I'll have the caprese salad if you please. And my friend here will have—" He grinned, showing off his smiley scars. "What'll it be, Wambach?"

"Arnold Palmer."

"An Arnold Palmer, then. Thank you kindly." He waved her off and grinned some more, this time at Wambach. "I'll put it on our tab. Our mutual employer can pick it up. Might as well enjoy the perks. And I tell you, friend, that's the glory of this nation. Back in Scotland, when I'm on a job, I'll be lucky if I get a bit of porridge as a perk. But here, oh, sweet mountains, there's so much to choose from. A lad could get himself spoiled, I tell you."

A muted grunt from Wambach. "I've learned to take my pleasures where I find them."

Mr. Grey snapped his fingers—alarmingly loud. "A man after my own heart. That's precisely my opinion." The waiter arrived with their food and the Arnold Palmer and puttered off. I forced my eyes into the brochure to make sure they didn't catch me looking.

Could only hope to the Woods those flowers did their job and covered my smell.

This mutual employer—the big money bankroll covering their tabs—that was interesting. Probably who hired Stinko and Daisy too. Who wanted Dr. Braithwaite followed. Were they here? I'd have to wait and see.

"I'd say that's enough small talk." Mr. Grey didn't bother with a fork—just hoisted up the plate and ushered a mass of juicy tomatoes, leaves, and chunks of mozzarella down his gullet. I glanced up from my brochure to watch it. Hell, I couldn't look away. "You've got the money, Wambach—so how about holding up your side of the bargain?" Gouts of tomato juice ran down from his scarred jaws, collecting in the curves of his carved smile.

"All good." Wambach pushed a key across the table. "Hardware's in a white-panel van parked across the street."

"Ain't that a wonder?" Mr. Grey stood. "You order something and get it delivered to you. You Americans love your comforts, don't you?" He pocketed it. "We'll be in touch, in case we want to order anything more—or if we need your services in another capacity." He hesitated. "Though, to be honest, I do have one question."

"Oh yeah?"

"That spiky tattoo on your hand, laddie—what's it mean?"

"Oh, this—the *Sonnenrad*?" I couldn't see it—until Wambach held it up—showing the inked spiky swirl imprinted on the back of his hand, running from wrist to fingers. "Black Sun. Just some ink I got a while back. A moment of youthful indiscretion, but you'd be surprised how many doors it opens." He settled back. "Don't knock it, Mr. Grey. America is the land of comfort—you're right about that. But you gotta make sure you have the right friends." Then he smiled.

A mountain lion smile.

Mr. Grey gave him a wave. "I'll keep it in mind. Good day to you, Mr. Wambach."

"Good day to you, Mr. Grey."

Black Sun. I knew the design, if not the exact meaning, from my short criminal career. It was Neo-Nazi stuff. There was some ideology behind it—which most humans detested. Or at least, pretended to. Something about one type of Harrower who styled themselves hunters in a world of prey. Another bizarre quirk of their species. More importantly, a lot of folks who followed that ideology turned to organized crime to fund it—or maybe they just liked breaking the law and used markings and a shared philosophy to bind them together. In any case, they were dangerous.

And they congregated around Grizzly Hill.

Mr. Grey started for the end of the veranda and Wambach left his seat. Which one to follow? I decided on Mr. Grey—he was easier to see at least. Already, he'd gone to a little shack and strip of pavement below the veranda and hopped into a golf cart laden with a big bag. Seeing him inside, hunched over with his arms jutting out, was like trying to watch a black bear ride a child's tricycle. I smiled a little.

But if I wanted to follow him, I had to hit the links myself.

I pocketed the brochure and left the veranda. Made a quick stop to glance at a set of regulations by the equipment checkout zone—putting my back to Mr. Grey—and then waved down a caddy. A flash of the guest pass got me a golf cart of my own and a set of clubs in a big bag.

The clerk, a kid with a mass of pimples, watched as I hoisted up one of the golf clubs. "Um—that's the wrong side." He gulped. "Would you like to wait for some other players so you can have a game?"

I tossed the club into the passenger seat and plopped down. "No thanks. I'll figure it out."

I got behind the wheel before he could reply. My foot didn't quite fit, and I sort of had to punch my heel against the gas pedal to make it go—which it did, nearly running over the clerk. "Sorry!" I hooted an apology, gripped the wheel with one hand, and sent the golf cart spinning to the side and onto the turf. One of the clubs tumbled out and flew into a hedge.

Fitting into this new sort of wilderness wasn't going to be easy.

I sent the golf cart rumbling along the green expanse, passing gentle, arched hills, pale stretches of sand and kidney-shaped lengths of water. Other golfers moved about, zooming along in their little carts, or strolling to the next hole in chatting clusters. Every so often, a golf club smacked down in a pleasing rush and sent a little ball skyward with a satisfying crack. They were playing in tamed nature—every bit of grass, every plant and drop of water arranged just so. The putting green was the worst of all. Nature distorted, twisted from its usual form into something that suited mankind perfectly.

Like a bigfoot living on fast food and takeout.

Up ahead, Mr. Grey's golf cart came to a halt. He parked next to another, where two other men worked their clubs. I parked as well—staying well-back. Picking a link two or three behind them. Couldn't eavesdrop—couldn't even get a good view—but it would stop me from getting noticed. That was the best I was gonna get.

I hopped out of the car, grabbed a mass of golf balls, and a few clubs, and went to a stretch of grass below the shade of a towering oak. Made a show of letting a golf ball plop down, picked a slim club, and gave it a few practice swings—then twisted around and whisked out my phone for a selfie.

Which just happened to get a perfect view of Mr. Grey and his friends.

I put on a huge smile, showing off my fangs—and zoomed in on the far link. The two other golfers were enjoying themselves. One was a bit older, his hair a puffy sheaf of silver and white. He wore a brilliant pink golf shirt and was laughing at some joke he had just told—patting the shoulder of the other guy. This one was younger, a little pudgy, with close-cropped orangey hair. Even though he had the gloves and the right clothes, the golf club looked awkward in his hands.

I gave the air a sniff. A particularly noxious cologne drifted across the course, emanating from White Hair. Far too sweet—like crushed-up dead flowers had been crammed up my nose. Even from here, I could smell it. Did the dude bathe in that perfume?

Probably something expensive. To have a membership to a place like this, to be able to pay for muscle like Mr. Grey and Wambach, you had to have the big bucks. They wanted Dr. Braithwaite followed, they wanted something purchased from Wambach, and they were using Mr. Grey as a go-between. Send the Scottish Mountain Man to do the dirty work while they kept their expensive hands clean. All that was clear as a blue California sky—but I needed some more puzzle pieces to complete the picture.

"Excuse me?" A pleasant voice from the edge of the grass. I looked over. A plump, middle-aged human in golf course finery—baggy trousers, argyle socks and vest, and absurd flat cap, came walking over to me, one of the club's caddies lurking behind him. "Pardon me there, friend—but uh, you look a little lost." He had a smiling, fleshy face with thick chipmunk cheeks. "For instance, you're only supposed to have one ball at a time."

"Oh yeah?" I'd dropped down a bunch. "Sorry. Didn't really have golf in the forest. Toss the Pinecone's more my speed." I glanced down the links. Mr. Grey and his friends had moved on—I was losing them. Chipmunk Cheeks was being nice, but he was keeping me from his targets.

"The name's Hal—be honored to show you the ropes." He held out his hand. "With those arms, sonny, I bet you've got a hell of a swing."

"That's okay." I reached down, collecting the golf balls. Too small—they slid from my fingers. Rolling on the grass. "Wouldn't want to disturb your game—"

"Oh, it's no trouble." He lunged down and caught one of the balls—moving surprisingly fast, and then whisked out a tee, bopped in front of me, and set it up. "I'm just putting in a little practice while the wife catches up on her gossip. I tell you, once you're retired, it's like you're in high school again." He laughed as he slid behind me, jabbing a club with a bulbous head into my hands. "Now this here is called the driver. Can be hard to handle for beginners, but with pythons like yours, I bet you'll do just fine."

Holy Woods—maybe if I played along with this guy he'd be satisfied and leave me alone. How many rules could golf have?

"And what does the driver do?" I asked.

"It sends that ball flying, silly." He stepped back and went to work his hands, prodding me into position. "All right. Feet apart. Hips back. Hands down—you've got to hunch, buddy, given your size—now pull back—and swing!"

I brought back the golf club. Clenched it tight. Frustration trickled in. Getting sprayed by Stinko—the clutter and mess in my condo—those Jefferson

Ranger clowns outside Milo's school—his worry when I nearly picked a fight. They coursed inside of me like salmon in a stream. I swung down, expelling breath in a grunt, and put every bit of bigfoot strength into the swing.

The club carved a furrow through the air. Sent a mass of grass—along with the golf ball—soaring into the air. I stepped back as grass and dirt rained from the sky, like I'd blasted the earth with a bomb. The little ball went soaring along, a white speck in the sky, before hurtling downward to a placid lake a few links ahead and vanishing with a splash.

It was right next to the green where Mr. Grey and his employers were working their putters. They all looked at me.

Hal slapped my back. "Whoo-whee! Will you look at that? Fantastic swing, buddy. You got the power, I'll say that again. We just gotta work on your aim."

I looked past him. Hardly hearing. Mr. Grey was heading over now, rolling his golf case along behind him. He was humming a little—some sort of jolly Scottish tune—and it trickled across the open grass. Behind him, his two friends had leapt into their golf cart and motored over to the next hole. Mr. Grey had his eyes fixed on me, a pout on his scarred lips. He was like a hawk above a rabbit. Just picking the right moment to swoop. What could I do? Dash into my own golf cart and motor out of there? I'd probably drive it into the sand.

Besides, sometimes a detective's gotta stop playing sneaky. Camouflage will only take you so far.

"Hello there!" Mr. Grey crossed onto the grass, clasping his hands. "I see you're giving my brother some pointers. You have my gratitude, sir—but I'll take it from here."

"He's your—ah—your brother?" Hal's eyes flicked between Mr. Grey and me. We had different fur coloration and vaguely different sizes.

"I'm speaking metaphorically. We're all brothers, aren't we?" He drew closer now, towering over Hal. "Go on and enjoy your day, friend. I'll handle the rest of the lesson."

I hadn't said anything. Hal seemed like a nice dude. Let him go on his way and then me and Mr. Grey could talk.

He shrugged, gave me a quick nod. "Just, ah, keep practicing your form there." Then he waddled away, his caddy trailing him.

Mr. Grey and I watched him depart. He crossed away from the shade of the tree and ambled toward the next hole. The seconds ticked past, and a tremor crept under my fur, but I didn't show it. Just looked back at Mr. Grey, matching his smile.

"You've got a name, then?" Mr. Grey asked. "Brother?"

"Arlo Patches." No point in hiding. No point in playing coy. "I'm a private investigator. What about you? You got a first name?"

"Aye—it's 'mister.'" He leaned down. "A detective, then? Makes sense. You were following me on the veranda and then over here. Were you following me before, perhaps? Maybe you think you're good at it." That smile came again, twisting up the scarred lips. "I'm *Am Fear Liath Mor.* We don't get followed—we do the following. Track you over the highland mountains, push you off a cliff."

I stared back. Like with any predator, you didn't show fear. "You weren't so hard to track. But Stinko and Daisy—man, tailing them was cub's play. They told me everything." I nodded down the golf course. "Did you hire them to get Dr. Braithwaite? Do your bosses know how badly you screwed up?" Pretending to know more than you did—classic PI move. "What about Wambach? I don't know how long you've been off those mountains, but most humans don't look kindly to those who run with Neo-Nazis."

He looked me over again. Sniffed deeply. "Let me show you something, Patches." Then walked back to his golf bag, which he'd parked in the shade of the tree.

I followed. Walking slow, arms tense—ready to throw down if needed. Mr. Grey got to his case and unzipped it. He reached down. "This is my driver." He drew out not a club—but a sword. A huge sword—a thick length of metal bigger than my arm, and sharp enough to take that limb off with a swing. Mr. Grey let it rest at his side, keeping the blade in the shadows. "It's a claymore. This arms dealer fellow had it, kept it in his mansion in the highlands along with all his goons. And me—in a wee cage. Ended up taking it. Along with plenty else. You ken my meaning, lad?"

"That's a nice sword," I said. "You know the Harrowers invented other weapons too? They call them guns."

"Oh? Is that so? I've got some of those too." He let the point aim in the dirt, flicked his fingers against the handle. "But believe me, Arlo Patches, if you want to follow me or Mr. Rusk again, it'll be my sword that finally does you in." He leaned closer, showing off those scars. "Now—go on and bolt."

I did—crammed myself into my golf cart and drove straight back to the clubhouse.

Mr. Grey had given me something he assumed I already had. A name. Rusk.

I crossed through the lobby. "Mr. Bark?" The clerk with the walnut up-do called out to me. "So, do you think Shambhala Sam will—"

"We'll be in touch!" I waved to her and made it to the parking lot.

Got behind the wheel of my pick-up and roared out of the country club parking lot. Just in case. A little bit of driving gave me the perfect place to stop—a Taco Bell parking lot. I whisked out the phone and started searching up Rusk. Dry biscuits, hair products—nothing I could use. I kept going, added

'California,' 'business,' 'politics,' to the mix.

Finally got something.

Lloyd Rusk. His picture matched the white-haired dude with the bad cologne I'd seen on the golf course. He even had a website for his business—Rusk Consulting. Austere black wallpaper and sleep-inducing explanatory text showed that Rusk finessed political operations for a vast assortment of clients. He knew governments, knew ordinances at the local, state, and federal level, and could make problems go away. Or at least, that was what I got from the corporate speak on the website. I've had easier times trying to decode birdsong.

He did, however, have a link to his social media account. I had a look.

Lloyd Rusk grinning behind a huge swordfish on a boat. Lloyd Rusk golfing with assorted political bigwigs, all flashing thumbs-up. Lloyd Rusk beaming behind a huge meal at some steakhouse, hoisting up a massive neon blue cocktail. Lloyd Rusk skydiving.

I guess the guy liked living large.

But as to who he was working for or why they'd want Dr. Braithwaite, I still didn't have a clue.

Up above, the October sun had started to set. Rosemary wanted me at that community meeting, and I wanted to be there. I'd lit the fuse by telling Kowalski to release the wolf photograph. Might as well see what damage I've done.

I gunned the engine and started driving—to the Taco Bell drive-thru. I could at least get some food on the way.

On the way back to Sarsaparilla Springs, I rung up Ramon to ask him to feed Patterson before the meeting—not knowing how long it would take. "No problem, man." He answered with a laugh, pleasant as always. "Actually, Jacob and I were gonna head to the meeting ourselves. Want to see the fireworks." I hooted back at him as I shoved a fistful of veggie quesadilla into my mouth. He probably wouldn't be disappointed.

Sure enough, the school parking lot was packed. It seemed like all of Sarsaparilla Springs was heading to the meeting. I worked the napkin over the stains, plopped on another layer of deodorant, and followed the line of locals inside. Halloween decorations—pumpkin-headed scarecrows—watched us as we entered. Kowalski walked ahead of me, hands in his pockets—looking nervous at the growing crowd. He and I exchanged nods and then he headed to join his wife on one side of the auditorium, and I ambled over to Rosemary and Milo.

The cub had a homemade sign, matching those hoisted up by several of his classmates. 'Save the Wolves' in big letters and a picture of a smiling wolf—though it looked more like an obese pale prairie dog.

"Uncle Arlo!" He hooted at me. "We were talking about wolves today, and I think I saw footprints outside the classroom, but Ms. Perry said they were from a possum, and then we were talking about how important the wolves are, and we made these signs and—"

Rosemary laughed. "Glad you made it, Arlo. Harold will be glad too. I think he's a little nervous."

At the front of the auditorium, right below the light-up scoreboard, the school principal and the mayor worked to set up a microphone. Static hit the air. Harold Patches shifted in uncomfortably in his seat.

My brother. Same sort of light brown fur as mine, and similar dark eyes. He was bigger—a little taller than me, a little bulkier. Way more mature. Right now, Harold wore his full sheriff's uniform. Khaki shirt, dark tie held in place with a pin, and even a Smokey the Bear broad-brimmed hat, which shaded his fuzzy face. He spotted me and nodded. Milo gave him a wave.

Another click of the microphone and Mayor Meyers, a portly woman in a pantsuit, waved Harold over. Evidently, Sheriff Bigfoot was gonna be the first up the trail.

"Thank you." He looked over the expanse of the audience, shifted a little, and grunted—making the static in the mic crackle. I could smell my big bro's nervousness. "Now, I want to be respectful of everyone's time for this informational meeting, so I'll explain the position that Nugget County Sheriff's Department holds about the newly arrived wildlife." A few hoots from squatch citizens and excited humans. "Wolves are—so it seems—back in this part of Northern California. I understand that ecologists have speculated about this for some time. Now, wolves offer great benefits to the environment—managing prey populations, stopping disease in deer herds by eating sick animals—and we're lucky to have them. But it's important that we—"

"Are you sure about that?" Eddie Jerome, Jefferson Ranger Sergeant-at-Arms, spoke up—more like shouted, calling out from the audience.

Mayor Meyers raised her voice. "We'll hear concerns from the public after the—"

Harold hooted. "No, no." He nodded Jerome's way. "Let him speak." That was my brother. He didn't want anyone to feel upset.

All eyes went to Jerome. He looked around nervously, scratched his nose, and then turned to Ollie Candle—I guess he liked making noise, but didn't actually want to speak. Candle sighed and glared at Jerome, who merely shrugged.

Then Candle stood. "Sheriff Patches, I just want to say that I respect you, I've voted for you, and you've always done a good job as sheriff—but this—this is not okay." His wife and Caitlin Candle sat next to him, both watching—and Caitlin didn't have a 'Save the Wolves' sign. "We're not talking about some new type of grouse. These are wolves. You don't have to say more than that."

Harold grunted. "I understand your concerns, but wolf attacks on humans are exceedingly rare."

Bringing up statistics? Oh, Harold. I could almost see the crowd's eyes glazing over.

"But it does happen." Candle spoke clearly and murmurs followed his words. "My daughter plays in the woods—she loves the outdoors, just like me. And I know your son does too. I have to ask, sir, with all due respect—when it comes to our kids, isn't any risk too much?"

You couldn't argue with that.

My brother lowered his eyes. "Mr. Candle, the likelihood of an attack is so low—"

"And then there's the matter of our livestock." Candle kept going, building momentum. The rest of the crowd was listening, those in Jefferson Ranger hats bobbing their heads. "I raise sheep and goats. A lot of my friends do too. Every animal that the wolves take down is a major hit to our bottom line—and with things being as tight as are, those are losses we can't afford."

Jerome chimed in. "And what if our ranch land gets turned into a nature preserve, and we get thrown the hell out? What about that?"

Many more agreeing murmurs now, and nodding heads, and a few smatters of applause. Rosemary made a worried hum and Milo shifted in his seat, looking at his father. His dark eyes shone. Poor guy. Trying to appease humans—they were stubborn as ticks once they got a hold of something.

"Folks, please—folks." Harold hoisted up a hand. The talking continued. Jerome was trying to get a 'No Wolves' chant going, and a few of the Rangers took him up on it. Their words echoed through the elementary school gym, and then a counter-chant started—'Save the Wolves.' The two sides recited their words, each trying to outdo the other in volume and vehemence. "If you'll just—if you'll just be quiet—" I could see the frustration building. Harold had worked to be civilized, to be the kind of bigfoot humans loved.

But even he had his limits.

He roared. A full-on bigfoot bellowing. The kind that made campers piss their sleeping bags if they heard it in the forest. The call rang against the walls of the gym and the chant and chatter died.

"Ahem." He cleared his throat. "Um—as I was saying." Becoming the polite elected representative again. "I understand your concerns. I really do. But I do have to say that, if you look at the statistics, predation's effect on livestock is extremely small. We already have Black Bears in Nugget County—we can live with wolves." Then he snorted. "And I'll say something else. I am a law enforcement officer. I will enforce the laws. And Grey Wolves are listed under the Endangered Species Act—so they will be protected."

Plenty more cheers went up for that. Rosemary and Milo clapped their hands vigorously, and so did I. A lot of the squatch citizens at the meeting added their howling, deep, booming calls echoing through the gym. Plenty of humans were clapping and cheering along too. I scanned the gym. Hard to tell how exactly the town was divided, but if I had to guess, I'd say that we had the anti-wolf brigade outnumbered—though not by much.

But for all of Harold's grand words, he hadn't talked at all about Candle's concerns.

Candle came to his feet. "You're not even listening to us. It's like we're not even there." His wife was saying something to him, but he was already walking away.

The other Rangers too. Jerome stepped into the aisle and spun around—wanted some more grandstanding. "Looks like we know what side you're on, sheriff—the critters that share your fur." He gave a final bow and followed the Rangers out.

That's when I smelled it—the noxious cologne that had infested the golf course.

I shifted in my seat, looking back at the door. Tracking the scent.

There he was—Lloyd Rusk. Now wearing a charcoal business suit, the kind of expensive that looked cheap. He reached out to Candle, offering his hand. Candle shook it.

Just when I thought I had a handle on this case, there was another twist in the trail.

We went to Harold and Rosemary's place after the meeting, which limped on for an hour more after that climax. I pulled up and Rosemary led me to the dining room, where Harold had shed some of his uniform and was relaxing with a sasquatch-sized mug of tea. Rosemary had put some Halloween decorations here as well—including a big printed photograph of a grape labeled 'this is a witch's eye.' I didn't have the heart to mention that it didn't exactly make sense.

Didn't want to mention Milo talking to the goat back at Rose's winery either. Harold looked like he had enough troubles.

Milo sat across from him, already swaying his seat—one tired cub. "They'll be okay, right?" he asked. "The wolves? And Caitlin's dad—they'll realize that the wolves aren't dangerous. Right?"

Harold patted his shoulder and hummed, and Milo drew closer. "We'll figure it out, buddy. Now, tonight's a school night—you better get to bed."

"It's not that late." He looked up at me for support—especially because, when I watched him, I regularly ignored prescribed bedtimes.

But this time, I could tell that Harold was upset. "Gotta follow the rules, furball." I picked up Harold's broad-brimmed hat from the table and put it on my head. "Hey, how about this for a Halloween costume? I'll be a cowboy—giddy up, little doggies!"

It made Milo smile—as much from embarrassment as amusement—and he headed out to his room.

Harold let out a rumbling sigh. "That—that didn't go well."

"It could've gone better." Rosemary sat next to him and plucked at the fur on his cheeks. Doing a little grooming—always a comfort. "They'll get it. They'll figure it out. They'll live with wolves, just like they live with bears and raccoons going through our garbage cans. Just like they've learned to live with us."

"Hmmm." He gave me a snort. "What do you think, Porcupine? Think they'll get used to it?"

"I'm not sure I'm used to it—especially since I'm involved." I started talking, telling him about why Walter Rose had hired me, and some of the interesting new specimens of homo sapiens that I'd bumped into today. Harold listened carefully, police officer instinct kicking in, while Rosemary looked alarmed. "Any info you can find on Mr. Grey, Wambach, and Lloyd Rusk—I'd appreciate it."

"Can do, can do." He scratched his chin. "So you asked the guy at the Bigfoot Museum to release the picture, huh? You're the spark that set the woods ablaze."

"Guilty as charged."

The doorbell rang. I glanced out the door. Two new vehicles had pulled into the driveway, out of place next to my old pick-up. A sleek Corolla, business-black, and behind that, a motorcycle. My sister and sister-in-law had arrived.

Rosemary opened the door and Harriet Patches entered. My little sister—she'd come up from Sacramento, where she was running the Sasquatch Political Action Committee, to join the fun up here. Her fur, same caramel as ours, rested under a neat blouse and blazer. "Sorry it took me so long. Came right from the office." She gave some nuzzles to Harold, Rosemary, and me.

"Okay if I take your guest room?"

"Our pleasure," Rosemary said. "Hello, Freshta."

Freshta stood silently in the doorway. Dark fur tinged with just a little gray—a barmanou, from the Afghanistan-Pakistan border. Black motorcycle jacket, the helmet tucked under an arm. She gave us a quiet nod. Freshta loved Harriet, that was plain to see—and she also scared me.

"I'd offer my place," I told Harriet. "But that would mean I'd have to clean it."

"Well, we wouldn't that." Harriet settled next to me. "You staying out of trouble, Porcupine?"

Harold laughed. "I wish I could say he was—he's responsible for this whole thing. Well, not exactly, but he got that wolf picture published and sent out to the whole wide world."

"Is that right?" Harriet's eyes shone, her teeth flashing in an amused smile.

"Yup." I let my hands fall limp to the table. "A guy had the picture and he asked me for advice—I told him to let out the wolves."

"Let out the wolves," Harriet repeated. "Well, Harold, you did the right thing. It'll be tough, I think, to protect these wolves, but when the Children of the Earth decided it was time to leave the forests and save this planet, we knew it would be tough. And if the alternative is the destruction of the environment—that's a fight worth fighting."

My little sister thought I had done the right thing. She'd always been the one to do that—while I did the opposite. She'd devoted her life to the cause of the Children and the planet.

Kind of nice that I was playing my part too.

Bigfoot Trap

We had breakfast as a family the next day, right at the Fat Fox Diner. It was good to be there and enjoy the food, without worrying about a case. The whole extended Patches Family—Harold and Rosemary, Milo between them, Harriet, and Freshta—and me. Between all our orders, we had the table creaking under the weight of short stacks, vast bowls of fruit, mountains of veggie sausage and bacon, and—my order—a baker's dozen of biscuits drowning in a mushroom gravy sea. They were playing Willie Nelson on the jukebox, the sun was shining, and all was right with the world.

Conversation drifted toward reminiscences, as it tends to when family gathers—human or squatch. Harriet had the floor. "So, Arlo—genius that he was—had been watching this batch of car campers since they arrived. I'm not

"FURBALL, DON'T DO ANYTHING THAT STUPID."

sure how, but he decided they'd be perfect for robbery."

I spooned a mass of drenched biscuits into my mouth. "Look, they left their snacks in their tents. Figured a nylon tent flap would save their goodies—they were asking for it." I pointed to Milo. "When you're camping, furball, don't do anything that stupid."

"I definitely won't." Milo grinned, syrup thick on the fur of his chin. "Did you rob them?"

"You seem rather excited about your uncle breaking the law," Harold said. "Should I be worried?"

"It's a good story!" Rosemary said. "Go on, Harriet. What happened?"

"I knew my big bro was up to something and I wanted to come along. He said no—but I ignored him." Somehow, Harriet hadn't gotten a single scrap of food on her t-shirt. Freshta sat next to her. Totally silent. "It was an old pattern we had. He'd insist on doing something stupid and I'd insist on going along. Good thing I did too."

"Why's that?" Milo asked.

I drained my coffee. Wasn't so proud of this next part. "Turns out their snacks weren't all they left behind."

"They had this dog—big one. Mean one." Harriet snapped her fingers. "What do you call them—I sometimes get confused, humans have so many breeds of dog. They really worked a number on that species. German name—pointy ears."

"Doberman Pinscher." Freshta spoke for the first time. Trace of an accent.

"That's it—a Doberman Pinscher. And it turns out they didn't even leash him up. Guess they figured he'd guard their stuff, which he did. Soon as Porcupine here unzips the tent and reaches in, Fido comes charging out looking to get his jaws into a Child of the Earth." She grinned at me. "I've never seen Arlo move so fast, big bag of potato chips in his arms as he crossed the campsite, the dog hard on his heels. Of course, I was scared too. Made it halfway up a tree, grabbed his arm, and pulled him along after me."

I grunted. "I seem to remember me pushing you up the tree before the dog got us both."

"In any case, there we were—treed. The Doberman was running around, barking like crazy, and we both knew it was only a matter of time until the family came back from their day hike and found the discovery of a lifetime."

"Did you try calming the dog down?" Milo asked. "Most animals aren't aggressive, once they know you're not a threat."

"You're one smart cookie, son." Harold patted Milo's back and he smiled. "But in this case, he'd already made up his mind."

Though maybe Milo could have calmed the dog down—like he had with the goat back in the winery. I settled back in my seat, wondering if I should mention it. Milo hadn't—and I didn't want to put him on the spot. It didn't feel right. Besides, Sheriff Harold Patches had enough on his plate, considering the community meeting last night hadn't exactly gone his way.

"What did help was that I got hungry." I patted my stomach. "So I cracked open those potato chips and started munching on them."

"Seriously?" Rosemary asked. "That was snack time for you?"

"What can I say? I'm a stress eater." I shrugged. "And good thing I did, because the fragments of chips rained down, right on top of the dog—and he started eating them. Gobbled them up so much that he stopped barking and bought Treetop and myself some time." Harriet grinned at me. "We crept down and made it out—just as the campers returned from their outing."

"Found the dog eating their potato chips." Harriet shook her head. "They were mad at him. I always felt guilty about that. It wasn't his fault."

"When I found out what happened—your fur was covered in potato chips fragments—I was plenty angry myself." Harold snorted. "You could have been killed. You could have been discovered—photographed. And for what? A bunch of chips."

"Sour Cream and Onion," I said. "They were pretty good."

Rosemary and Milo hooted at that. Even Freshta seemed amused, with a slight smile that reminded me of a line etched in bark. That might be the best I was going to get out of her.

Rosemary took Milo to pick something out on the jukebox after that, leaving us to handle the check and discuss business. Harold calculated the tip while I showed Harriet the picture of Lloyd Rusk from his website. "He's involved in this Braithwaite thing. Up to his neck. And he was at the meeting last night—went right up to Ollie Candle, guy who runs the Jefferson Rangers."

"Rusk." Harriet flashed teeth as her dark eyes shone. Same response as if she'd seen a rattlesnake. "Yeah, I know him."

"That good, huh?"

"He's a class act, a political operative who loves the high life. Early career working behind the scenes in Sacramento. Assembly, State Senate, governor's office. Then he went private, offering his services to the highest bidder in almost every field. Lately, it's been environmental policy. California's got a host of regulations, and he walks his clients through all of them, making sure they adhere to the letter—but not the spirit—of every bylaw, and never lose a shred of profit." Harriet handed me back my phone. "Rusk is smart. He knows how to play the media, how to stay out of trouble, and he gets results by any means necessary."

"So the two of you have clashed?" Harold asked, worry in his deep voice.

"Now and then. It's a tossup as to who won which skirmish." She shrugged. "If he's in Nugget County, he's working for a client. He's not here for the scenery."

The waiter showed up, collecting Harold's credit card—and Eddie Jerome was right behind him. He had on full Jefferson Ranger regalia—the ballcap with the symbol, hunting camo jacket, and a scowl to go with it. Two other Rangers stood behind him, backing up their pal—both with their cell phones raised to film the interaction: Man Versus Beast. Rosemary and Milo came back a moment later, and she clutched his hand, her arm going protectively to his shoulder.

For a few seconds, everyone just stared at each other. Harold gave them a smile. "Can I help you?"

"You're wearing that uniform, huh? After what you said last night?" Jerome asked. He seemed plenty nervous now—the fear smell bursting from him in a sudden wave of stink. "Ought to take it off if you're gonna throw the good people of this town to the wolves."

"We can talk about this later," Harold said. "When my family isn't here."

Jerome's eyes went back to the cellphones. It looked like there was nothing he wanted more—but he was being recorded. "Well—what about—what about the families of ranchers and farmers? Who now have to fear packs of wolves lurking in their backyards? It seems like you care more about the forest where you used to live then the town you're in charge of defending."

Then the jukebox started playing something. Weird Al Yankovic—Eat It. Ridiculous lyrics. Long lists of food. Had to be Milo's pick. My neighbor Ramon had been playing Weird Al for Milo when we took him to see some superhero flick a few weeks ago, and he loved it.

"So—so why don't you—" Jerome stopped. Squinted in the direction of the jukebox and fell silent.

You couldn't have a showdown with a novelty song in the background.

Harold emerged from his seat. Towered over Jerome. He touched the brim of his hat. "Have a nice day, Mr. Jerome."

But as we stood, I glanced over at Freshta. She clutched a knife, right at her side. The blade angled down, her grip tight—a soldier's grip. I never quite knew Freshta's background—how a barmanou from the highlands of Afghanistan had made her way to the United States—but she clearly had a warrior's instinct. Harold was a calm and placid pond, and I doubted Jerome was a threat, but if the situation got worse, I wondered if she'd work that knife between Jerome's ribs or across his throat.

Saved by Weird Al.

The Rangers slid away, letting us pass, and we went outside to our trio of cars. Harold passed me a folder as Harriet and Rosemary traded nuzzles. "File on your friend Wambach," he explained. "It's not exactly light reading. You be careful, Arlo. I figured this job would be easy when I passed it to you, but if it isn't—if you want to stop—"

"Stop when you've got Harrowers like—" I stopped myself as Harold let out an angry chuff. He didn't like that word—especially when Milo could hear. "People like Sergeant-at-Arms Jerome going against us? Not a chance."

"That's what I thought, Porcupine." He leaned closer and patted my shoulder. "Be smart."

"Will do." I set the file on my passenger seat and hopped behind the wheel.

Political power players creeping in from Sacramento. My brother, getting insulted during a family breakfast. What was happening to Sarsaparilla Springs? I knew the answer—someone had let out the wolves.

I cruised home and flipped through Wambach's file while Patterson munched Fancy Feast. He emptied his bowl and then went straight to my belly, posting up above my belly button, and letting out piteous meows. Some creatures are never satisfied. I plopped him next to me and gave him some pets while I read. It seemed like Wambach had some trouble with self-control as well.

Aggravated assault. Criminal conspiracy. Grand larceny. And that was just the half of it.

He'd been born in Sarsaparilla Springs, in and out of state institutions since before he could shave—falling in with the Aryan Brotherhood during a short stretch in Folsom. Got released, thickened his jacket, and went in again—this time for half a decade. Since then, he'd bounced around between various groups—including some seriously hardcore armed robbers in Oregon—before settling with a low-rent outfit called the Volk Vanguard in Grizzly Hill. But the dude had learned. Could always cut a deal, find a fall guy, or make sure a witness vanished to keep him breathing free.

Tough criminals were a dime a dozen. Smart criminals were rare—and far more dangerous.

I let the folder settle on my coffee table next to the growing tower of pizza boxes. What deal did Wambach have with Lloyd Rusk? No wonder Rusk was using Mr. Grey as a go-between. That Grey Man brute was another nasty mystery. I could ask my big bro for his file, but I doubted the local sheriff's department would have much on him. Maybe I ought to try the FBI—or Interpol.

I stood up, Patterson taking that as his cue to drop down from the couch and tangle himself between my legs. What was the best move? Maybe swing back to Terroir Valley and see if I could sniff out Rusk? But that would mean crossing paths with Mr. Grey, and I wasn't in a mood to do that.

Then my phone rang. Except, it wasn't mine. The ring tone wasn't the chirping cricket noise that I'd picked because it reminded me of childhood nights in the woods. Instead, this phone was a booming country song with a thunderous club beat—one of Stinko's hits. "Gucci on a gator—Balmain on a bullfrog—" Repeated over and over again in an autotuned drawl.

Holy Woods—who was calling up Stinko?

I stumbled back to the kitchenette where I'd left Stinko's phone plugged in and had a look at caller ID—a pic of Daisy wrapped in a heart. I opened it up. Telling a lie wouldn't work. Daisy presumably knew what her lover's voice sounded like. "Yeah?"

"Arlo—hey." Stinko, not Daisy. Sounded like he'd just run a marathon—or was looking down the barrel of something dangerous. "Thank the swamp. You gotta help me, man. When I signed up, it was for a simple tail job. Daisy and me had picked up some heat in Frisco, we figured the northern woods were the perfect place to hang out. It's bigfoot country, right? We didn't expect that we'd—"

Words like rabbits running from predator jaws. "Easy there." I went to grab my coat—which Patterson had chosen as the perfect place to lay. "First of all, are you safe?"

"Yeah—for now." A spray of whines. "But we're being followed. It's Wambach! Those Nazi dudes are on us like mosquitos. Now, Daisy and I will throw down. I'm not afraid of anything." I didn't bother calling him on that lie. "But they got us outnumbered. We need some evac, bro—and you're the only person I know."

"Okay—I'll come to you. Are you in public?"

"Yeah, I figured that was smart. We're at Captain Jack's—the casino?"

I knew it. Captain Jack's Hotel and Casino, right at the edge of the Snake River Indian Reservation. Amazing how many of my cases ended there—parents sending me to find their kid who they feared had vanished into the forest, trying to live wild, when he was really parked in the casino, sucking back complimentary drinks as he fed quarters into the slot machines. Since it was Saturday, the place probably had a decent crowd.

"Stay put. I'll meet you there."

"You better hurry, man. I'm keeping it together, thinking tactical—gotta be strong for Daisy, you know?"

"Sure. Should be there in twenty minutes. Can you hold it together for that long?"

"Yeah—you got it." He swallowed. "Arlo—thank you."

"Don't mention it." I hung up and went to the door. If Stinko was about to tangle with the Vanguard, we needed serious firepower—except I didn't have any. Harold was very clear that if I wanted to stay free, I couldn't own a firearm. I'd make do. The forest had already given me plenty of weapons. Thick fists at the end of each arm. Sharp teeth for slicing vegetation that could do the same for flesh. Harrowers had better look out.

I opened the door, only to find Harriet waiting for me. She had a sleek trench coat over her pantsuit, hand frozen—just about to knock. "Arlo—there you are!" Behind her, Freshta leaned against her motorcycle, arms folded. "Arlo—I got a job for you. Should be a piece of cake for my master detective big brother."

"Count me in—but not now." I hoisted Stinko's phone—figured I'd bring it along to return it. "Skunk ape friends of mine needs help. They're connected to the case. May have worked for our friend Rusk."

A familiar glow flashed in Harriet's eyes—firefly-bright. "Can I come along?" The same look she showed all those years when I wanted to raid a campsite for potato chips and she wouldn't be left behind. This could be a major problem.

"I'm afraid not, Treetop." I smiled back. "Might be a little dangerous." Changing the subject might help. "What do you need?"

"Jefferson Rangers are having a meeting tonight at the house of their current Grand Marshall—Oliver Candle. I take it you're familiar?"

I crossed over to my pick-up. "Should ask Milo. He and Candle's daughter worked on the same science project." I was busy, but there was no way I'd turn her down. Harriet didn't deserve that. Even if spending the evening with the Jefferson Rangers wasn't how I wanted to wind down the day. "I'll swing by. See what they're talking about. Who knows? Maybe they'll do some barbecuing. I'll see if they can cook me up a veggie burger."

She flared her nostrils and snorted. "You're still taking risks, Porcupine. Still sneaking around campsites."

I got behind the wheel and waved to her and Freshta. "I'm a detective now. That's my job."

Then I sped away, Johnny Cash's deep growl on the radio as I started the drive to the Snake River Reservation. No need to speed. If Stinko stayed in public and didn't do anything stupid, he'd be okay. Stinko not doing something stupid—might as well ask a squirrel not to bury acorns. Thankfully, the drive wasn't long. A hop across the freeway and then I rolled into the Reservation. The casino waited—a big glassy lump squatting amongst the trees.

I parked and headed in. A big statue of Captain Jack himself—some Modoc rebel hero—hoisting up a sword as if he might start slicing away at the senior citizen junkets and buffet-hungry tourists swarming past him and into the casino. I joined the crowd. Blue velvet carpet soft against my feet and silver salmon decorations swimming along the walls and hanging from the ceiling. Amongst the retirees in windbreakers and walkers, I stood out like a sequoia amongst wind-bent birch. Hopefully, Stinko and Daisy would too.

Sure enough, I spotted them as soon as I entered the cavernous main room—both at the Blackjack table. Stinko was playing, his fear forgotten, looking at the cards over his designer shades. Daisy sat on the stool next to him, sipping from a massive drink the color of an overripe mango.

And their predators weren't hard to spot either.

Just across from them, working on the slots. Two shaved heads, one scrawny guy in a beaten denim jacket, the other in a lumpy sweater. Both played the machines—but their eyes stayed fixed on Stinko and Daisy. Reminded me of rangy coyotes, licking their chops at the promise of a meal.

I watched them through a mirrored wall and walked to the Blackjack table.

Stinko was arguing with the dealer. "Bro—why am I losing? I scored like a twenty-eight, or maybe a twenty-nine. That's the highest number here!"

Daisy's feathery tail drooped. "Honey, no. That's not how it works. You've got to get twenty-one, or close to twenty-one as possible. If you get higher—"

"That doesn't make sense. It's a game, I got the high score—I win." He looked back, noticing me for the first time. "Arlo, help me out here." He waved to the dealer, some high schooler in a blue vest and bowtie who looked like he didn't want to argue with a skunk ape and a bigfoot. "Tell this fine gentleman how games work."

I looked around the table. Wrinkled old timers and chubby tourists. "Apologies, folks." Then I clapped a hand on Stinko's shoulder. "You're gonna have to do the next round without him." They didn't seem broken up about it. "Tip the dealer, Stinko—and let's go."

He flipped a chip in the dealer's direction, and we walked amongst the tables. I steered them away from the corner of the slots, where the Nazi duo had shifted in their seats. They'd certainly clocked me—but were they wise to the fact that I'd done the same to them?

Stinko, heedless as always, pushed up his sunglasses and beamed at me. "Arlo—thank you. I knew I could count on you. Didn't I say that, Daisy? That Arlo Patches could be counted on?"

"Sure did." She took another slurp on her straw and sucked up the last of her drink. "But he's gonna want some quid pro quo for this, I bet." The same phrase Kowalski had used.

I stopped. "First off, I'm still a little raw about you spraying me. I've showered about a billion times and the stink's not quite fading, so how about you cool it? And secondly—yeah, I want something. Some information."

"You got it, bro." Stinko bobbed his head. "I want Daisy safe. We'll go into witness protection, I'll wear a wire—whatever it takes."

She rolled her eyes at that, but still drew closer and gave him a nuzzle, and he clasped her furry paw and held it up to his heart. They loved each other, no doubt about that, and Stinko was willing to turn snitch to keep her safe. Looking at them was like looking at a big-eyed chipmunk or a faun—I had a sudden urge to protect them.

I hummed low. "I'm a private detective. I can't put you into witness protection. Can't give you immunity or anything like that."

"But you can get us out of here?" Daisy asked.

"That, I think I can do. You got a car?"

"Badass Ferrari, man," Stinko said. "Waiting outside."

"The Vanguard knows about it—better leave it here. You can pick it up later. We'll take my pick-up." I went to a hulking game with a supersized screen. Some reflection in the swirling patterns dancing around the words urging players to 'win big.' The two Nazis had left their seats and trailed behind us, Lumpy Sweater brushing past a cocktail waitress trying to give him a free drink. I wanted them out of the way, and I wanted to leave without taking the main entrance. Did this place have a back entrance? I looked past the buffet. Big doors leading to the kitchen. Had to have a way out through there.

Holy Woods—why was the detective business so hard?

"Come on. We'll cut through the kitchen." I squared my shoulders, trying to go authoritative. "In the meantime, tell me what you were doing, searching for Dr. Braithwaite."

"That's just it—we were only supposed to tail her." Stinko shrugged. "That's not illegal. Is it? It was Mr. Grey who hired us, this big Scottish bigfoot. Kooky accent, but he was a nice dude. Loved to party. He hooked us up with Wambach. We were supposed to bring Wambach the details of where Braithwaite was going, where she was camping, how her research was going—that sort of thing. And for maybe a week, everything worked great."

Daisy snorted. "Until Stinko decided to start filming a music video."

"Hey, man—'Spark the Redwood' was gonna be a major hit." Stinko sighed. "So, she caught wind of it and ran, and we lost her in the woods. I'm from the Everglades, bro—I don't do forests. And I kind of avoided telling it to Wambach, so now he's sent some guys to watch us."

"Might do more than watch." We reached the kitchen. Stinko hadn't told me much I didn't already know, but I could dig into that later. For now, I had some skunk apes I needed to save. I brushed through the doors and entered the kitchen—a couple chefs working at their stations, dicing vegetables, working pans—busy as bees to keep dishes flowing to the buffet. A lean guy with a neat beard, his toque at an angle, stared at me like I'd descended from a flying saucer.

I guess they weren't used to bigfeet in the kitchen.

I flashed my business card. "How you doing? I'm Bobby Bark, food critic for Boone Appetit, a magazine celebrating the wilderness-based culinary world. You mind if we have a look around?"

Stinko was already jabbing his face at a tray laden with dough waiting to be rolled. "Oh man, I wish I had my phone. Posts about food always do numbers."

Then the door swung open behind us and any pretense of a lie vanished. The two Volk Vanguard goons swarmed in, both flashing pistols. "Everybody not covered in fur get the hell out!" The scrawny dude in denim swiveled his gun back and forth and the kitchen staff got the message—huddling together and scrambling their way amongst the counters and racks and toward the alcove with the freezers. A smart decision. Couldn't say the same for the Nazi Twins.

"Go on and get Patches—the squatch in the cowboy shirt." Denim Jacket gave the orders.

Lumpy Sweater looked like he was gonna vomit right there in the kitchen. "Jesus, Skinny—do I gotta?"

"You got a goddamn .45, Pomeroy—that makes them a whole lot smaller."

Pomeroy swallowed and started toward me—gun extended. That big pistol bought him some courage and bigfoot or not, it could punch a round through me that would do real damage. I glanced at Stinko and Daisy, my eyes going to the back. A service entrance leading to the sun-washed parking lot. Daisy took my meaning, even as Stinko mouthed his confusion.

By then, Pomeroy was close enough to give my fur a pet. I didn't look at the gun—stared at the face behind it. A few pimples, stubble from a recent shave. Swastika tattoo poking up from his collar, small enough to be mostly covered—like he was embarrassed by it. He was like a deer, ready to run at the first scent of danger. Fine by me.

I grunted. A nasty sasquatch noise that made him stumble—and then I grabbed the pan of frying salmon next to him and gave it a flick that sent a mass of fish and oil into Pomeroy's wide face. The sizzling fish bounced against his nose, the oil stung him, and he wailing and gasped and flailed his arms—and didn't shoot me.

I struck first, slamming a furry fist right into his belly—just below the ribs so it sent all the air rushing out of him. Put enough muscle into the blow to take his combat boots off the floor and send him crashing down in a sputtering mass. His pistol tumbled away, falling into a sink—rattling against the stainless steel.

Skinny hoisted his automatic—going for a shot. I grabbed the rolling pin next to me and chucked it at him. It was the hefty marble sort and crashed against his sternum and sent him stumbling back. He made a noise like a belching bullfrog. Stinko and Daisy were dashing for the door, crashing their way through the kitchen, but I didn't watch. Raced through the kitchen instead and neared Skinny as he fumbled for the fallen piece with his offhand. Got a hold of his bald skull and introduced it to the counter—leaving a residue of blood against the metal.

As he dropped, Pomeroy was making it back to his feet. I crossed the kitchen, grabbed the steel door of a cabinet, and opened it—banging it against his head as well. The clank ran through the kitchen, he groaned, and dropped.

Then I exhaled. Next to me, a plate of baby tomatoes and lettuce waited. I grabbed a mass and popped it in my mouth. Chewed hungrily.

"Arlo?" Daisy's voice. I turned to the door.

She stood next to Stinko—both with their arms raised. Three more Volk Vanguard goons close behind—and these guys didn't look like the clowns who I'd laid out in the kitchen. Ski-masks, black-leather jackets. Shotguns. One of them had thick arms and I caught the Sonnenrad etched on the back of his hand.

Wambach.

"Outside." He aimed the shotgun straight at me—and there was no deer in him at all. "Try anything and I'll take out your knee and you'll have to crawl." No surprise as he aimed the shotgun at me. He knew I'd be there. He was expecting it.

Letting Stinko and Daisy see their tail. Seeing if they'd turn tail at the first sign of trouble and call me—their only friend in town. Then snapping us all up. It was perfect, with the cold intelligence that the worst of humans could summon up for their use. How do you bait a trap for a bigfoot? Simple. You use another bigfoot to lure him in.

And I'd taken the bait.

They herded us into a white panel van outside. No pillowcases or blindfolds—not a good sign. They didn't mind that we were seeing where we were going because our next stop would be a shallow grave. Wambach settled into the passenger seat and swiveled around, pointing the shotgun at us as his buddy drove. Highway and trees blurring by as we rumbled through light traffic.

Stinko summoned up what bravado he had. "We ain't scared of you, man!" He shook his tail and flashed teeth. "Sure you got muscle, and some scary tattoos, and—and a lot of guns—but I'm from the Everglades. Ain't nothing scares me!"

I rolled over, trying to get comfortable. "Don't waste your breath. Don't get him mad."

Wambach pulled his ski-mask away. "I'm not mad." He reached out with the shotgun, letting the muzzle settle almost gently on Stinko's belly. "And I don't care if you're scared of me or not." I looked at his eyes, a vibrant, brilliant blue, and wished I hadn't.

There are certain things in the forest—a sky split with storm, lightning in terrible flashes, a forest fire crackling and flaring, an avalanche rushing down a mountain slope—that are incapable of compassion or mercy or pause. Wambach was like that.

A pure killer, who looked at us as problems to be solved.

I forced my eyes away. He hadn't killed us yet. I could only think of one reason why—the Volk Vanguard wanted to figure out how much we knew, who we'd talked to—what next steps to take. Then they'd take care of us.

Come sunset, I might be in the ground. I'd never see my family again. Harold's guileless trust, Harriet's pluck, Rosemary's love, and Milo's boundless kindness. But what really got to me was Patterson. It wouldn't make sense to that chubby cat that I wouldn't be there tonight to give him his dinner.

Holy Woods, that hurt.

Well, that settled it. I wasn't dying out here.

The van door rolled back. We were on Grizzly Hill—right in the middle. A little cabin perched on a slight rise, surrounded by towering trees. People here liked their privacy. Some Volk Vanguard boys stood guard—if that's what you called relaxing in Adirondack chairs and cooking marshmallows over a decorative stand-up firepit. Rifles leaning next to them as they rested their skewers over the flames. No Nazi flags, but there were a few Halloween decorations. A big inflatable witch stirred up a glowing cauldron, some ceramic zombies clambered out of the earth, and a set of pumpkins waited by the front door, already carved into Jack-o-Lanterns. I got to look at them all as Wambach frog-marched Stinko, Daisy, and me up to the porch.

Another skinhead opened the door. He had a sweater vest and a set of square, black-rimmed glasses: the substitute teacher from the Third Reich. He looked at Wambach distastefully and led us to a cozy little den where three folding chairs waited. The place didn't exactly look like Hitler's bunker. An assortment of dolls sat on the mantlepiece. Little figurines in a glass display case. 'Live, Laugh, Love' and 'Bless This Mess' in block letters mounted on the wall. They sat us down and went to work—using chains and padlocks instead of rope.

Just wanting to be sure.

A woman entered from the kitchen, sipping coffee. She had blonde hair veined with gray in a neat bun and wore a cable-knit sweater. "So." She took a big drink. "You're the two sasquatches that have been causing all this trouble, yeah?"

"Skunk apes," Daisy said.

"Yeah," I said. "I'm the sasquatch. Arlo Patches."

"Oh, I know who you are." She gave me a quick hint of a smile, making laugh lines shift. "I'm Brenda Stull. I'm running the Volk Vanguard while my husband's taking a federal vacay." She walked over to me and leaned down—just a little—to look me in the eye. "And let me tell you, Mr. Patches—it is not easy."

"Who knew running a White Supremacist criminal organization would be so hard?"

"You have no idea." She sighed. "Oh, we got supporters. Just pop on the internet and you'll find them. But that's the problem. These kids will type and type about the Great Replacement and sneak Fourteens and Eighty-Eights into their posts until the cows come home, but when it's time to actually do something—or even donate cash to my husband's legal defense fund—then it's a different story."

So it was all about money—big surprise. That's how it always was with Harrowers.

"You need cash. Is that why you went to work with Lloyd Rusk?"

Stull took another sip of her coffee. A long one. Probably gathering her thoughts. "You know about that, huh? You happened to have mentioned it to your big brother, by chance?"

"Maybe it'll come up—right after I tell him where Dr. Josephine Braithwaite is."

Baiting a trap for humans wasn't so hard. You just had to find out what they wanted. It was our only chance.

Wambach sucked teeth. "He's lying."

I was. "She's right in the forest. Camped away. You think anyone knows the State Park better than me?" I leaned back, trying to get comfortable—or at least look comfortable. Not easy to do with a thick length of chain wrapped around my wrists and another around my ankles. "You let me and the skunk apes go and I can show you where she is. Then we pass the info along to Rusk and split the proceeds." Delaying tactic. Anything to buy a few more seconds. "That's why you're doing this, right? Make some money—or are you more about the cause?"

"Well, what's good for the goose." She stared into her coffee, thinking it over.

"You'd really lead us to Dr. Braithwaite?"

Was she buying it? "Look, I'm a squatch, okay? As far as I'm concerned, this is a human argument. I got paid to be involved. If I get paid more by Rusk, I'm perfectly willing to switch sides." I gave her my best friendly wood ape smile. "You can understand that, can't you?"

She thought for a few moments, then nodded slowly. "Untie them."

"What?" Wambach demanded.

"I gotta repeat myself? Untie him and Stinko. Then put him in the van and let him take you to Dr. Braithwaite."

Stinko nodded—then froze. "What about Daisy?"

"Daisy?" Stull walked over to her. She hadn't said a word this whole time, but kept her face in a permanent silent snarl. "Oh, she's my insurance. Just in case you don't deliver, I'll go to work on her." She smiled. "Maybe I'll skin her. Turn her into a new winter coat. Make that tail into a feather duster. What do you think of that, Daisy?"

Daisy showed her a mouthful of fangs. "I'm going to unload my stink glands into your face."

"What a charmer." She clapped her hands. "All right, time's a-wasting. Wambach, get these two in the van. Stanley, take the boys out front and go with them. Go right to the woods. That way, in case Mr. Patches is lying, there's plenty of places to put him. It's a big forest, and bigfeet are good at staying hidden, aren't they?"

Stanley had drawn a pistol-grip shotgun leaning below the Love Lives Here sign. "You heard her, Wambach. Let's go."

He didn't say anything, but knelt low and went to work with the keys. Bicycle chains went from our legs to our wrists. "Thanks." I grinned at Wambach. He didn't smile back. He did the same to Stinko, who reached over and nuzzled Daisy. She hummed a little, a gentle sound, and then Wambach jabbed his shotgun in Stinko's back and pushed him in my direction. Toward the door.

Daisy stayed. It hurt Stinko like a cougar's claws.

We went outside, back in the fall air. Some of the Nazis looked up from their s'more-making and watched us as we crossed to the van.

"You guys ought to be on our side." Stanley started pontificating while Wambach went ahead to the van. "Did you know that the Third Reich launched an expedition to Tibet to try and locate the Abominable Snowman? They believed he was the Proto-Aryan, the link to the birth of the White Race. And you guys—you're closely related to yetis, right?"

"Yeah," I said. "Closer to yetis than you—and glad of it. Ain't that right, Stinko?"

...WAMBACH WENT AHEAD TO THE VAN.

For once Stinko was silent. Then he looked at me, with sad eyes. "She was against this, you know. Against coming here. She tried to talk me out of it. She always does. But she sticks with me, even though my dumb decisions just put us in deeper and deeper water. I don't know why. I really don't."

"She loves you," I said. "Simple as that."

"Yeah." Stinko's eyes went to the sky, now washed with dark clouds. The Autumn night, rolling in early. "I wish I deserved it."

"Okay." Stanley—maybe upset that we didn't like his Proto-Aryan theory—cut in front of us and pointed to the van. "Get inside. You first, Stinko, and then—"

Then his shotgun clanged loudly and tumbled from his arms. He dropped, screaming.

The echo of the shot, a sniper rifle's terrible crack, split the still air and for a long, long second there was nothing but crackling flames from the firepit, and then the flutter of wings as a flight of birds lifted and zoomed skyward.

The goons behind us woke up. Dropped their s'mores fixings, went for their guns, and started toward us. Wambach had the shotgun out and aimed at the trees, fired, racked it, and shot again. Probably wishing he had something with more range, cursing himself for letting this trap swing shut.

"It's coming from the woods!" He pointed to the line of trees across from us. "Put some suppressing fire on him!"

The sniper fired again, blasting one of the legs off the firepit. It tilted over, hurling burning logs and sparks onto the skinhead assemblage.

Giving Stinko and me a chance. I decided to take it.

Stinko was darting back to the house—going for Daisy. A big mistake.

"Stinko—come on!" I worked at the chains. My arms strained. Managed to slip one hand through the loop and then I shook the coil off and sent it rattling to the floor.

Then I grabbed Stinko's shoulder and pulled him along. Running for the forest. Anyone sending shots whistling at the Pottery Barn Third Reich had to be a friend. I pulled Stinko ahead, stopping to grab one of those lawn zombies on the way and bring it down on Wambach's head. The ceramic shattered and he crumpled to the grass—but his eyes stayed open and glared at me hatefully. Didn't give him time to look before I scooped up Stanley's fallen shotgun, bashed him with the butt, and booked it for the forest.

We reached the shelter of the trees as more shots roared around us—the s'mores contingent finally getting everything together and pulling their guns. Pistol pops and something automatic chattering away. Stinko and I scrambled amongst the trees as bullets hummed down, ripping free chunks of bark and shattering branches.

Seeing some trees getting shot didn't make me feel any better.

I pressed my back to a tree, looked ahead—and Holy Woods, there was my pick-up. What the hell?

The branches above shook. Freshta descended. She had a sniper rifle clasped in one furry arm.

"Arlo." That's when I noticed her motorcycle resting in the back of my pick-up. She slung the rifle over her shoulder and hurried back, taking care to stay low. "Get in. Your spare key's in the ignition." I always kept that spare in the glove box in case I needed to give the car to someone else. Good choice. "Let's go."

I grunted. "What are you doing here?"

"I followed you. Let's go." Spoken like she was inviting me to go and get a sandwich. She pulled the motorcycle free, grunting a little with the weight. Stinko and I helped and we got it out of the truck bed and onto the pine-needle strewn soil—even as more bullets cut the air. "Thanks—now follow me out."

I scrambled into the cab of the pick-up as she righted her motorcycle. Stinko slid in and looked at me. His pleading gaze said it all.

Daisy. She was still in there.

Good sense told me to put the pick-up in reverse and follow Freshta straight out of there. But I put it in drive instead. "Holy Woods." I looked at Stinko as he tugged free of the chains and gave him the pump-action. "Buckle-up."

He smiled, the gold and gems in his teeth making his grin shine like the sun. "Hell yes."

Then I slammed my heavy foot on the gas pedal, and we went roaring out through the trees, blasting like a stampeding herd of elk straight for the cabin.

We cut through the road. I didn't bother with the driveway—not that there was much control as the engine churned up gravel and grass. We roared across the lawn. Grass sprayed everywhere. That big inflatable witch bent down over the hood, giving the windshield a kiss with her green lips, and then she popped, deflated, and went under the wheels. The Nazi goons were next, pausing in their gunfire to dive for cover and avoid the front bumper.

I drove right up to the front door. Smashed it straight through. Took that door down and a good deal of the porch walls as well—punching straight through plaster.

Inside, Daisy—still chained to the chair. She saw us and smiled—more at Stinko than me. Stull was next to her, a revolver held at her side. She plastered on a false smile—arm tensing. "Now, hold on just a moment—" Going to put that gun on Daisy.

The shotgun roared, blasting the air above her. "Drop it." Stinko hissed.

She did and raised her hands.

Stinko tossed me the shotgun and scrambled out. He dashed across the cutesy living room and ran to Daisy. Some hooting, some grunting, and the chains slipped free from her legs and arms. She started back—and I was counting the seconds. How long until the skinheads by the porch started shooting up the car? Or—the real danger—Wambach standing up, finding a gun, and finishing the job himself?

"All of you are gonna die." Stull gave us a smile. "Daisy, Stinko—you went ahead and turned yourselves into loose ends that gotta be tied off. And Mr. Patches? You involved yourselves in our business. You don't get to walk away from that."

Daisy reached the edge of the pick-up and gripped the dented metal rim. "We're from Florida, honey. You can't scare us."

Then she lifted herself on one leg, twisted around a little, and put her stink glands to use. Sending a gout of snot-green fluid lancing the air in a shimmering arc and giving Stull an emerald paint job. Stull tumbled back and dropped into her cozy armchair, right below the 'Live, Laugh, Love' sign. Then Daisy hopped into the truck bed, and I put the pick-up in reverse.

I peeled out hard. Roared into the driveway. A shotgun roared, punching a shell into the cab. A spider-web appeared in the windshield and ripped out the back window. Wambach stood, a spare shotgun in his hands. He racked the pump and fired again as I put the pick-up in drive and slammed on the gas. Daisy hooted. Stinko hooted. We flew down the road, Freshta zooming ahead on her motorcycle, and roared down Grizzly Hill and to the safety of the freeway.

I was hooting too.

My condo seemed like a natural place to go after the near escape. I brought the pick-up—bullet-ridden, with cracks in the windshield—up to the driveway and we all piled out. Stinko and Daisy, arms around each other, and Freshta staying close to me as I unlocked the door. "Sorry for the mess." I led them inside—knowing that an apology wasn't much compared to the stains and garbage that ruled my current habitat.

Stinko spread his arms and dropped down on the couch. "You kidding? This place rules."

Patterson came out, eager to greet the guests. "And who's this?" Daisy swept him up, giving him the pets that he craved and making him purr.

While they relaxed, I slid in front of Freshta. She had plopped a sort of suitcase on my kitchen table—shoving a bunch of old beer cans to the floor with a sweep of her arm. Then she started disassembling the sniper rifle, unscrewing the pieces, and setting them in their proper place in the padding with practiced speed. I sat across from her. "You were following me?"

"Harriet asked me to. A good thing I did."

So Treetop wasn't tagging along. Instead, she sent her girlfriend to protect me. "Where'd you learn to shoot like that?"

"YPG, in Syria. People's Defense Units." The names were familiar. Something on the news, several years ago—but humans always seemed to be slaughtering each other somewhere. Freshta freed the sniper scope from its moorings and placed it neatly in the case. "If the Kurds saw what happened today, they would have been amused."

"It was amusing?"

"It was sloppy. I should have killed all the Volk Vanguard, but Harriet made me promise not to take any lives." She settled back. "I'll report to her at your brother's house after this. Will you attend the Jefferson Ranger meeting, as she asked?"

She looked like she was daring me to refuse. "Of course."

"Good. You can report to Harriet tomorrow." She finished with the rifle and closed her suitcase. "I'll see you, then."

"Freshta." I hummed. "You did save my life today. Thank you."

"Hmmm." She made a curt grunt and started for the door.

She probably thought I was plenty amusing myself. Or sloppy. Her girlfriend's ne'er-do-well brother-in-law, who had gotten in over his head and needed bailing out. And everything I'd done that day had done nothing to change her mind. Maybe that was the story of my life, bumping from one screw-up to another, and relying on my family to pull my fat from the fire.

But at least I had Freshta watching my back. And Harriet's back as well.

I followed her to the living room, where Stinko had reclaimed his phone. "Arlo, what do you want for dinner? We ought to go all out to celebrate surviving. I'm thinking something fancy. Applebee's. My treat."

"And then what?"

"Figure we'll stay here." He made his eyes puppy-dog big. "Well—where else are we gonna go, man?"

"I don't know. The police, for protection. A motel."

Daisy was still petting Patterson. "We go to a motel, the Vanguard could find us. And the cops—you know we can't do that. Not with all those warrants out on us."

"Misunderstandings," Stinko said. "Nothing serious. But we don't really have time to explain."

Holy Woods—these two were like an ant infestation. "The Vanguard could find you here, you know. And you do realize my brother is the sheriff."

"That's why it's perfect—the Vanguard wouldn't dare risk an attack on the sheriff's brother!" Stinko beamed—proud of his smarts. "And as for your big bro, maybe don't tell him where we're staying?"

I groaned. But the swampland duo had a point. Cutting them loose was the same as leaving them for dead. Stull would have her goons prowling Nugget County, trying to sniff out skunk ape. They'd relay the information to Rusk as well, and he'd have Mr. Grey join in the hunt. The smart play, of course, was to turn them over to my brother. Harold could give them nice accommodations in the county jail while law enforcement agencies from a dozen states fought for custody.

But I didn't want that. Stinko and Daisy hadn't done anything worse than I had done. The difference was that I had a brother working in law enforcement, who kept me out of trouble and forced me to keep my muzzle clean.

We had gobbled down too much of the modern world. My skunk ape friends had choked on it.

"Applebee's it is," I said. "But there's some ground rules—you gotta be quiet, you can't leave, can't do anything that could give the game away. You got it?"

"No worries." Stinko bobbed his head. "We'll order delivery."

Great.

Then he looked up from the baby back ribs and chicken tenders on the Applebee's menu and stared at me, all the good humor and bravado seeping out of his eyes. He glanced back at Daisy—she was busy rubbing Patterson's tummy. "Arlo—what you did back there—what you're doing now—it means a lot." He held out his fist, bracelets clinking. "I've never had many friends. Even back in the swamp days, I stood out. You don't have to be so nice to us. But you are."

"Means I'm a fool, huh?"

"No." His eyes sparkled. "It means you're my friend."

I took his hand and clasped it.

Friends—can't say I had them in abundance.

"Let me see that phone," I said. "I'm starving."

One Applebee's meal later—I stuffed my belly with glazed veggie riblets—I took the pick-up out again. I'd have to take it to a garage sooner or later, see what they could do about the dents and the plaster crusted on the hood—not to mention the bullet holes. In the meantime, I cruised through Sarsaparilla Springs and into the countryside. Out back to the ranches carved into forest meadows. The Jefferson Rangers social media gave me the address: Candlewick Ranch. Ollie Candle's place.

FREE STATE OF JEFFERSON HERE I COME.

I drove through an evening darkened with fall shadows. Tall trees on all sides, only the occasional gleam of headlights—and then, after a turn, the ranch itself. Big gravel driveway below an old-fashioned arch decorated with antlers. At the end, a long, flat, rambling ranch house, and green fields beyond that where the goats would graze. Empty right now, apart from moonlight. But I couldn't say the same about the ranch.

Numerous cars had parked in the gravel. Men in Jefferson Rangers ballcaps ambled inside, eager for the meeting. Eddie Jerome played doorman.

Soon as he saw me, he lowered his clipboard and gave me a glare. "Turn your hairy ass around and—"

"Whoa, whoa." I held out my hands—going non-threatening. "The meeting's open to the public, ain't it? Everyone in Nugget County, according to the posting. Isn't that right?"

"How do I know you won't report everything you hear to your brother?"

"Up to something illegal, Sergeant-at-Arms?"

"Eddie!" Candle's voice came from inside. "Let him in."

Jerome stepped aside, giving me the same look he would give to a wild wolf crossing the doormat. I grinned back at him and walked inside. Comfortable furnishings, a plump couch, armchairs, family pictures on the wall. Mostly occupied by Jefferson Rangers and other locals. Ollie Candle's wife—what was her name?—was passing out pigs-in-a-blanket and young Caitlin was also in attendance, talking amiably with the Rangers.

She spotted me and came right over. "You're Milo's uncle, aren't you?"

I had found a folding chair and was debating if it would hold my weight. "Guilty as charged."

"We had to do an assignment where we wrote about a relative that inspired us, and he wrote about you." He had? He hadn't told me. A sudden burst of pride, warm as the sun, settled under my fur. "He said that you used to rob banks. Is that true?"

"Um." The warm feeling vanished. I didn't want to discuss my criminal history with a fourth grader. "That was one of the things I robbed."

"Cool." Then her grin faded. "Do you think—do you think after this is over—that Milo will still want to be friends?"

"What do you mean by 'after this is over'?"

Then Candle cleared his throat. No microphone for him. The other guests fell silent. "All right, I'm officially calling this meeting to order. As Grand Marshal, I'll be overseeing the proceedings." The Rangers faced him, listening intently. "I'd like to start by talking about the bake sale we had last week. We had a decent amount of profit, and it was a good time—all that baking. I think making it a biannual thing could be a good idea."

The Rangers stared at him. They didn't want to hear about the bake sale.

"Well, ah, our first order of business—the wolves." Candle looked a little sheepish. "I've been doing some research. There are a few potential methods of keeping wolves away from livestock, same as they were in the old days. The ranchers and farmers up north, and over in Montana, Colorado—they've faced this problem and found countermeasures. Matter of fact, I've ordered one—should be delivered shortly."

Not much response. These guys didn't want to learn to live with wolves any more than they wanted to talk about bake sales.

They wanted the wolves gone. They wanted action.

Candle was smart enough to realize it. "And there's someone else I'd like to introduce. A new friend, who has agreed to help us—who knows about this sort of thing." He waved to the back of the crowd as a familiar cologne scent permeated the air. "Please give a warm Jefferson Ranger welcome to Lloyd Rusk."

Rusk walked right up. The bad penny, turning up again.

Free State of Jefferson

A smattering of applause. Rusk held up his hands and they went silent. "Evening, all. Good evening to you." He had an easy conversational manner to his speech like he was, as a human would say, 'chewing the fat.' "Now, I'm a stranger amongst you. Sacramento bigwig, I know, I know. But before you reach for your pitchforks and torches, why don't you hear me out?" He'd ditched the business suit as well, going for a simple collared shirt and khakis. No outdoorsman clothes—probably because he knew the Jefferson Rangers would sniff out an outsider in LL Bean camouflage. "You see, I sympathize with you. I really do. And I know how to help."

I scanned the crowd. The Rangers listened in. Rusk had their attention.

"Because, I'll be bluntly honest here—the government doesn't care about you. Politicians care about two things—votes and money. Big cities have both and get to run roughshod over places that don't. What you do have is wilderness, and that's what all your San Francisco and LA types like to turn into postcards. Want to come out here, see some actual dirt. They've paved over all their own, haven't they?"

He was working the crowd and getting a few nods. Hell, he was making some sense to me. I'd visited San Francisco a few times, during my wayward youth. The place was a nightmare.

"So now, you've got the wolves. And believe me—those are just what a lot of those city people are waiting for. Wolves eating your livestock is just part of the problem. You shoot one in self-defense, or the defense of your children and—bam—you're breaking the law and they take your land. They're itching to turn this whole place into a nature preserve. No hunting, no fishing, and absolutely no farming. Sorry, boys—you're out of luck. Now your home's gone because some rich man wants to go on a wolf safari. Call it ballot box biology."

Was that true, or was Rusk just scaremongering? Either way, it seemed to be working. There wasn't a creature on earth that didn't want to protect their habitat. "Want to complain? Too bad. You're an animal-hater in a state that loves its critters. Even more than people, it sometimes seems."

He paused, savoring the drama. A natural storyteller.

Candle swallowed. "That's, ah, rather bleak, Mr. Rusk. But you said you had a solution."

"Lloyd, please. And the reason I get hired, Ollie, is because I'm a straight shooter." He made a finger gun. "And I'm going to give you guys some bullets. Two of them."

The Rangers exchanged glances, nodding along. He had them.

"First off is the ballot box. California's a one-party state, but that's okay. Even if the state legislature won't touch this, we can still get it through—something called a ballot initiative." He reached to the table behind him and picked up a clipboard. "Maybe you seen these types outside of grocery stores, collecting signatures. They're doing that job because it works. Get enough signatures, get the measure on the ballot, and if enough people vote for it on election day, it'll pass. Direct democracy. Avoid the whole Sacramento circus."

Jerome was listening carefully, nodding his head. "So we gotta ask people to vote against wolves?"

"That's a good point. You see, that won't fly. Especially not in California, where they love their cuddly critters." He passed the clipboard to Candle. "So you do it in a way that doesn't mention wolves directly. People might like animals, but they like innovation, economic growth, and prosperity even more. Hell, they like having places to live that won't cost an arm and a leg. We're in a housing crisis—I'm sure you've heard of it." He folded his arms. "So, the ballot initiative, Prop 33, it'll be called, and what it'll do is create the Northern California Development Corridor. The NCDC—got a nice ring to it. Open the area up to development. Shave a little off the National Forest, bring in business. And as for the wolves, like our Big Bad friend in the picture..." He winked. "Construction noises will have him huffing and puffing somewhere else. Or at least that's the explanation that'll make the most sense when he up and disappears."

The clipboard went from hand to hand, a pen with it. Collecting signatures. I watched it go—far from surprised. Humans—Harrowers—liked the wilderness, right up until the moment it became inconvenient. Rusk was preaching to the choir, of course. He'd get a room's worth of signatures. But would others sign up? I didn't know.

Then, the clipboard went to a pair of gray shaggy hands. I looked up. It was Mr. Grey, smiling his extended scar-faced smile. He passed it on with a grunt. "Not a citizen of your fair country, I'm afraid." Then his eyes met mine.

I glared back, even as rattlesnake venom dripped into my heart.

"You said you had two bullets for us." Candle's eyes flickered. "What's the second?" He was worried—but still listening.

"Direct democracy. That's an American tradition. But there is another, one that staunch defenders of liberty have used from the days of George Washington to Martin Luther King." Rusk popped a leg up on a chair. Trying to look noble. "I'm talking about civil disobedience. You want to put a bullhorn up to your cause, you want to get headlines, you want support pouring in from across the state, hell, the whole country—because you better believe you're not the only ones who feel this way—then it requires action." He faced the crowd. "Do you hear me?"

"Yeah!" Jerome led the shout.

"I don't know what it'll be—I'm a stranger here—but I bet you do. So let's start thinking of something. Let's follow our rebel traditions." He pointed to the Rangers. "You are Sagebrush Rebels! Am I right?" Cheers of agreement and a great deal of clapping. "Then it's time for the rebellion to begin!"

The cheers went up in volume. The Jefferson Rangers stomped their feet. A few tossed their ballcaps into the air. I stayed seated—my eyes going to Candle. He wasn't cheering. Looked like he'd just gulped down a little venom himself.

Not that I was feeling much better. I'd set this whole mess in motion by telling Kowalski to post the wolf picture. Now, the state forest might get sliced up and these Rangers were going to turn their words into action. It was like in the old stories the band told you late at night—you wander astray, the hungry spirits and monsters will get you. I'd broken the rules, but it would be the forest that paid the price.

The meeting quieted down after that, the Rangers gathering in little knots to discuss their plans. Jerome and Candle were right in the middle of it. I wouldn't be invited in, and I'd seen all I needed. Time to head out, to plan my next move—before Mr. Grey made his. Except that when I stood up, Mr. Grey was waiting for me, his huge arms folded.

He gave me another smile, running his tongue along the enlarged edges of his scarred smile. "Mr. Patches! I was wondering if I'd see you again. Was rather hoping I would." He put a huge hand on my shoulder—a giant gray tarantula. "Come along. Let me show you around." His grip increased and up I went. I could shove his hand off and maybe drive a punch into his jaw, but that might send the wrong message to the Rangers.

Instead, I followed him out of the living room and into the little parlor by the porch. A deer's head rested there, a good ten pointer. That buck probably thought he was the king of the world until Candle or one of his relatives drilled a bullet through his heart.

I knew how he felt.

"I was just leaving," I said.

"No, no." Mr. Grey drew closer—uncomfortably closer. "Stay awhile. We go outside, perhaps. Take a walk in the moonlight. Though you might find that a wee bit difficult once I'm done slicing off your legs."

Well, if it was gonna be like that… "Why wait?" I flashed my teeth to match his. "Why not start right here?"

Then that cologne smell flashed closer. I looked up. It was Rusk. "Mr. Grey—please." He had the same bland smile. His younger friend, who still wore Armani, stood a little behind him. "I'd like to talk to our friend here."

"Sir, he—"

"That'll be all, Mr. Grey," Rusk said. Mr. Grey snorted at me and stepped back—still smiling. Rusk drew closer, his eyes going up to match mine. "Apologies. I know you're just doing your job. That's all we can do, right? We have our ideologies, our family, our backgrounds, and then we try our best. Sometimes you win, sometimes you just have to play out the string. I get it." He reached past me, patting the muzzle of the mounted buck. "I'd like you to meet someone. Hamilton, come and say hello."

"Hello." The younger guy emerged, brushing back fashionably floppy hair.

"Hamilton Hamlin Junior's dad runs HamCo. You heard of that? Real estate, development, resource extraction, energy—you name it, they do it. And they do it well." Rusk was going on and on while Hamilton Hamlin stared into space. Hamilton Hamlin Junior probably wasn't Rusk's friend—it was hard to imagine that softy, pudgy fellow joining Rusk for a sky-diving session. Which meant that he was Rusk's client. "And he'd love to meet with your sister and SPAC."

That was interesting. "Why's that?"

Rusk answered for him. "HamCo cares about the environment. Hamilton here's spearheading a brand spanking new green initiative, far better for Mother Earth than your rinky-dink state park, as part of the NCDC. I bet Ms. Harriet Patches wouldn't want to miss out on that—and she won't, if you decide to play ball."

Trying to buy me off through Harriet. I shrugged. At least they weren't handing me over to Mr. Grey. I could take Mr. Grey—maybe—but I didn't want to risk it. This was a way out. "Sure. Give me a business card and I'll pass it on."

"Please, take one of mine." Rusk had a sleek obsidian card already set onto my palm. Against my hand, it looked like a battle flag for ants. "We'll be in touch."

"Uh-huh." I pocketed the card. "Mr. Rusk—"

"Lloyd, please. I keep telling people."

"Lloyd—what are you doing here?"

His false smile vanished for just a moment. He had hawk's eyes—fixed straight on me. "I'm just enjoying the scenery, man. I love the redwoods." Then he was leading Hamilton Hamlin away and back into the living room where he could commiserate with the Jefferson Rangers.

He was dangerous. That was for sure.

I started for the door. Best to leave in case Rusk changed his mind and sent Mr. Grey after me. My hand was on the door when I heard gentle voices coming from the kitchen. A quick sniff revealed warm smells of baking and the earthy scent of a happy dog. I hesitated, peering into the kitchen. I could say that eavesdropping wasn't a habit for me, but I'd be lying. I was a detective, at least. Spying on people was my profession.

Inside, Caitlin Candle sat on a stool by the counter, her mother pouring her a glass of milk. Their dog, an Australian Shepherd, sat respectfully on his haunches. Caitlin stared at the milk. "He's going to do something bad, isn't he? He's going to get in trouble."

Her mom went next to her, pulling in close—the same sort of care that Rosemary showed to Milo. "It'll work out, honey. I'll stop him before he does anything too crazy. And he's just trying to protect us. That's what the Rangers do." But she didn't sound convinced.

Neither was Caitlin. "They do, I suppose—but then that Rusk guy was talking, and inspiring them, and they got all excited. It's like at school, when one girl says that I can't play with them, and then all the others join in. They just want to go with the group. Even if some of the kids in that group are my friends." She sighed. "Mr. Rusk—Lloyd—doesn't care about them, even if he said he did. He's making the Rangers do something because he wants them to do it."

Smart kid.

I could have gone in—could have introduced myself to Mrs. Candle and seen if I could glean any more information from her about her husband's plans.

But I'd caused enough trouble. Bothered that family enough. I walked outside, into night air a tinge too chilly to be comfortable and started the drive home. They were a nice family. Caitlin was Milo's friend. But now, more and more, I got the feeling that we were on separate sides.

Few cars on the road now. Fall leaves stirred and danced as I drove home. I reached my house.

Flashing lights. Roars and gunfire noises coming from outside the door. My hand tensed on the doorknob. I flung it open.

Just a movie on my big screen. A werewolf in an old-timey military uniform, unloading a machine gun as he howled. Watching the flick, their huge hands full of popcorn, were Stinko and Daisy. Patterson perched between them, his eyes reflecting the screen's glow. But Ramon was with them too, popcorn crumbs on his Dragonball Z shirt.

I grabbed the remote from the coffee table and punched pause. The werewolf froze. "What in the Holy Woods are you doing?"

Ramon instantly knew something was wrong and winced. Stinko just smiled. "Horror movie marathon, bro. Your neighbor's got every *World War Werewolf* film on DVD. We're almost done with the third film, *Alpine Lupines*. It's fire."

"Arlo—I'm sorry." Ramon was already standing up. "I met Stinko at the liquor store and—"

"You went to the liquor store?" I roared and it made Ramon wince. Then I stopped. Breathed in air. "Ramon, it's not your fault. You were just being a good guy." I pointed to Stinko. "But this skunk ape's supposed to be laying low. Not endangering my neighbors. Not going to the liquor store—"

Daisy hoisted up a six pack of glassy bottles as a peace offering. "We got you something."

"They're craft beers," Stinko added.

I tore them from her hands. The glass cool against my palm. The liquid inviting. The sort of bittersweet joy you couldn't find in the wild. I had many vices and drinking had to be somewhere near the top. After what had happened lately, the bottle was a relief. I used my fangs to pop the cap, sending it spinning away. It bounced off the coffee table with a click that sent Patterson scurrying away.

I pointed to Daisy and Stinko. "Lay low. Or we'll all be hunted."

Then I went to my room to finish the bottles. After a while, the sounds of the werewolf movie returned.

I woke up with a bit of a hangover. Burn the Forest, it was a bad one. The cause wasn't so much from the six pack of craft beers I'd downed, one after the other, but the couple of pints of vodka and some Old Crow that I'd used as a chaser. My mouth felt like a sun-washed prairie. Just a spark would make it burn. My head ached. I slipped on one of my Big and Tall cowboy shirts and jeans, checked my phone—Harold wanted me to come by his house—and started out.

Reminded me of the old days.

When I was working with my crew—me and Maple and some other bigfeet and humans. We tore through California in search of easy money. We'd hit a bank, kick up our share, and spend the rest on partying and guns. The human world just seemed so fun, bursting with color and delight, like a fantastic forest that you could dance through forever, laughing as the money rained down.

Except, that forest had its dangers as well.

Where were the others now? Dead. Jail. On the run. Or, like Maple, just plain disappeared.

And I'd been saved from that fate, because of my brother.

I drove to his house now, after swallowing about a billion aspirins, and devoured a package of breath mints for breakfast. Maybe that would hide away the red flags. Their neighborhood had the kind of quiet stillness that you only got on Sunday mornings. I gave the door a knock. No response, though I could hear motion and anxious conversation past the door.

Then Milo opened. "Hello, Uncle Arlo." He smiled nervously. "Um—it's good you're here. Everyone's sort of upset about something. I'm not sure. Something going on in the forest, I think." Most people would think that I'd make a bad situation worse—but not Milo. I was grateful for it and followed him in.

Everyone had gathered around the kitchen table. Harold had his sheriff's uniform half-on, working the buttons. His phone rested on the table, on speaker. Wayne Miller—the chief ranger at the State Forest—was on the line. "So, that's about the size of it. Figured I'd call you before doing anything else. Are you coming down?"

"I'll be there," Harold agreed. "Keep your distance. Are you armed, by chance?"

"...WHAT DID THEY TALK ABOUT LAST NIGHT...?"

"I could be. Should I bring a piece along?"

"No. Less chance of anyone making a mistake that way." He already had his gun belt on. "Sit tight, Wayne. I'm on my way." Then he hung up and looked at me. "Miller was coming in to open the park when he spotted men at the visitor's center. Bunch of trucks parked there, and guys with Jefferson Ranger hats. And guns. Lots of guns."

Harriet closed her eyes. "What did they talk about at that meeting last night, Porcupine?"

I fought through hangover brain fog. "Collecting signatures for some ballot initiative. And then something else. Civil disobedience."

Milo spoke up. "Well, that's not too bad, right? That's just, like, a protest. Like the one we went to in front of the state capitol. Right?"

Except people protesting to save the baby seals, the polar bears, and the planet typically didn't bring firearms to the picket line.

Rosemary put her hand on Milo's shoulder. "It's a little different. This is an occupation. It's happened before."

"Happened in Oregon," Harold muttered. "Turned into a forest-burning circus." He caught himself and grunted. "Apologies for the language. I heard horror stories at a law enforcement officer conference a while back. The problem is the media—and the people they summon. An occupation becomes a magnet for everyone who has an axe to grind. I'm not so much worried about the locals, but the out-of-towners they'll attract." His eyes went to his wife, the dark amber flickering with worry. "I don't want to scare you, but during the standoff in Oregon, the occupiers and their supporters would follow and harass families of local law enforcement."

"Holy Woods." Rosemary moaned. "Will we be okay?"

Freshta spoke up. "You'll be okay." Dead serious, as always.

"She'll stay here," Harriet said. "I'll go up with you and—"

"Sorry, Treetop—Arlo and me only." Harold smiled sadly. "You do good work, but you could be a target as well. Hunker down here, okay? I'll send a squad car over a little later." But I doubt they'd need it. Not with Freshta around. "Arlo, you good to go?"

Nothing like having my face shoved in the mess I'd made. I nodded. "Yeah, all right. Should I bring a weapon? It sounds like they're armed."

Harold sighed and gave Milo a nuzzle. "Look, most folks around here have firearms—the Rangers especially. Doesn't mean they're looking for a fight." The hope in his voice, the willingness to believe in the best of people, was bright as birdsong. "Hold down the fort, Milo. Okay?"

"Okay." The cub's voice was quiet. "Is Caitlin's dad involved?"

"We'll see."

Then we headed outside, Harold taking his sheriff's department car. I followed in my pick-up. If Harold noticed the damage to the bumper, he didn't say anything. I trailed after him, rolling from the suburbs to the highway and up to the Charles E. Boles State Forest. This was where we'd grown up, in the shadows of Redwoods and by the shores of trickling creeks. The last of the Children of the Earth to be raised in the wild. The same scents of loam and rot and distant pine, the birdsong creeping in over Waylon's voice on the radio. I'd been back, now and then, and the memories hit me like a pouncing mountain lion.

The two of us went to the deserted parking lot by the ranger's station and the toll booth. Miller stood outside. Dark skin, spectacles, a khaki and muted green uniform. We joined him. He eyed me—we'd had a few run-ins over the years. Then he fell into step beside Harold. I guess he decided that two bigfoots on his side were better than one.

"Checked the cameras outside the entry booth." Miller talked to us as we crossed the leaf-strewn parking lot. We passed familiar wilderness bric-a-brac. Carved wooden signs, a picnic table, information stand telling you not to feed the black bears. "Nothing. So I think they came in through the forest, using the trails on the Snake River Reservation. I called up Tribal Police Chief Woodrow Bondurant. He should be here momentarily."

"Hopefully, we can tell him that there's nothing to worry about," Harold said. "That all the Rangers have gone home."

"Don't count on it, Squirrel," I said. "At their meeting last night, they sounded damned determined."

Miller stared at Harold. "Your real name's Squirrel?"

Harold shrugged. "Yup." He stepped past Miller—taking point. We turned the corner, and the visitor's center rested right ahead in a little clearing. "All right. Just stay calm. I'll do the talking."

The visitor's center was a two-story square structure that looked a little like a giant milk carton. Big windows looked at the tops of the trees. There'd be dusty fake animals, Indian artifacts, historical dioramas, and more inside. I'd taken Milo there now and then, and when I was a cub, I'd sneak in and try to steal sodas from the machine in the corner.

Now, the Jefferson Rangers had claimed it.

They'd run the Double Cross and Gold Pan banner up on the flagpole, right below the American flag. Set up a bunch of fancy tents and their trucks and SUVs on the parking lot. They'd even busted out a camp stove by the picnic tables and were cooking up breakfast. Bacon and sausage smells came drifting across the lawn, just as they saw us.

All of them were armed—and not with the usual hunting guns either. This batch of long guns looked more suitable for fighting a war than anything else.

Eddie Jerome came hustling over, an assault rifle dripping in expensive attachments at his side. He stumbled a little, the monster gun awkward in its shoulder strap. "That's far enough, friends," he called. "This is the sovereign Free State of Jefferson. You hold no authority here."

"Damn it, Jerome—that's not—we're not seceding from the United States here." Candle joined him. He had a hunting shotgun slung over his back. "Hello, Sheriff Patches."

"Hello, Mr. Candle," Harold said. "Nice morning, huh? Good fall weather."

"Very crisp, sheriff," Candle agreed.

"That it is. I'm excited for Halloween—Milo certainly is. I bet Caitlin is too." He was being nice. Bonding with Candle. A good move. "So, would you mind telling me what you're doing out here?"

"This a protest. Civil disobedience."

"We're following the example of the Sons of the Liberty and Martin Luther King to tell the world the truth about what's going on here," Jerome added. "Farmers are being sold out to wolves and environmentalists. Big Government running amok. We're taking a stand."

The other Rangers formed a semi-circle around him, all armed as well. If a gunfight started, we'd certainly lose.

"You're having a peaceful protest?" Miller asked. "With guns?"

"We got a right to defend ourselves, don't we?" Jerome asked. "Or are you gonna take that away too?"

Harold moaned. A mix of fatigue and misery. "You need to stop this, Candle. Put your guns away. Pack your friends up and go home."

"Are you going to arrest us?" Candle asked. "Are we breaking any laws? Doing anything illegal?"

"No—that's not—" Harold stopped. "I'm not speaking as a law enforcement officer here. I'm speaking as a fellow parent. A citizen of Sarsaparilla Springs. A friend. If you do this, it's going to get attention."

"That's the point of a protest, sheriff."

"The media will turn it into a circus. Outsiders will come pouring in, looking to make trouble. Bigger, meaner, nastier agencies with lots of letters in their names will get involved." He removed his hat. Trying to look small maybe, which was hard for a bigfoot to do. "Somebody could get hurt. You don't want that, any more than I do."

"We're prepared for anything." Jerome patted his fancy gun. "The flowers of liberty require the watering can of patriots."

Candle glared at him. Something was up with Jerome—something beyond the usual wannabe guerilla bravado. Every time the flames died down, he reached for the gasoline.

And this whole business was rotten as a decomposing stump.

"You're stooges," I said. He stared at me. Harold too. "Stooges for Lloyd Rusk and Hamilton Hamlin. I'm not sure why. Not yet. But I know he doesn't care about you. You think he came out of here with some billionaire brat out of the goodness of his heart? He's using you."

But that was the wrong thing to say. Candle looked back at his Rangers—his friends—and then at me. "We're here because we choose to be. Now either arrest us or tell us that you're changing the policy that will let us keep the wolves from the door. I know you can't do that, Sheriff Patches, but this is bigger than us—this is about our families and our way of life. Maybe you don't understand that, but it's true." He raised his voice. "And we'll do whatever it takes to defend our homes and our families."

Cheers from the Rangers. Raised fists and rifles.

Harold gave me the look a mama bear would throw at a misbehaving cub. We started back.

In the parking lot, more police cars had shown up. Harold gave them a few commands, having two of his deputies stand guard at the trailhead. But we weren't alone. A pair of cars from the Snake River Reservation pulled in. The Tribal Police Chief, Bondurant, emerged, giving me some serious side-eye. We gathered at the picnic table and Harold spread out a map of the woods. Everyone exchanged handshakes.

"You brought your brother?" Woodrow Bondurant, an older guy, had a paunch pushing at his uniform. He wore his own Stetson, with a feather in the brim, and seemed almost amused at my presence. "I want him for questioning regarding a fracas at Captain Jack's the other day. If we got time."

"Arlo's studied the Jefferson Rangers," Harold explained. "He knows them."

"I think we all do," Miller said. "They're breaking the law. I'm not sure which one, but I'm pretty sure you can't take over a state park. The question is, what are we going to do about it?"

"Can't force them out." Harold grunted—speaking up before I could even make the suggestion. "All those weapons? It'd be a bloodbath."

"It's funny." Bondurant removed his cap. "I was at Standing Rock and then over in Michigan. Pipeline protests. The police came out with water cannons and riot gear. But when this bunch decides to declare war on the state government, everyone's walking on eggshells. Darn confusing." He smiled with false good humor. "But I hear you, Patches. Nobody needs to die. Do you have an alternative?"

"We starve them out," Miller suggested. "They can't get supplies in through the main road. Pretty soon, they'll get hungry. Tired. Bored. They'll want to go back to indoor heating and plumbing. We just have to wait them out until they decide their point's been made and they go home."

A siege. It made the most sense, even if it forced us to be more patient than them. I looked back at the trees. "We gotta make sure they can't sneak in supplies the ways they came. Through the Park. That's a lot of forest to cover."

"Good thing I'm a sasquatch," Harold said. "I know the woods."

"Where'd they get all those firearms, that's what I want to know," Miller said. "I know this is America, but some of those rifles..." He trailed off.

When I was hitting banks, that was the sort of thing I would carry—and only because of the connections our crew had. Maybe it had something to do with Harold's case in Grizzly Hill.

"I might have an idea," I said. The Volk Vanguard—Wambach, giving that key to Mr. Grey at the country club. "Give me some more time. I could give you some evidence, throw some legal weight on the Rangers and—"

Another engine's growl cut through the quiet. We looked up from our little council of war as a sleek Town Car came puttering smoothly over the gravel. Two more followed it and a large van too. Luxury car ducklings. They rattled to a halt in the center of the parking lot, doors snapping open in tandem. A small army of men and women in bright blue windbreakers. They had big letters—DOWM—stenciled on the back. The windbreaker crew spread out like hard working ants, marching everywhere to get food for the nest.

One headed right for us, badge already out. "Sheriff Harold Patches—I'm Special Agent Rod Todd with the Department of Wilderness Management." He had a protruding chin with a cleft a squirrel could use for burying acorns. Every part of him, from his crisply parted hair cut to his tie, looked like it had been designed in a lab. He jabbed the badge at Harold. We looked at it. Yeah—Rod Todd was indeed his name.

"Ah, good morning, Special Agent Todd." Harold looked at the edge of the parking lot. The DOWM boys had plopped down sawhorses and strewn out yellow tape. Some of them made for the trees, toting rifles. "What agency did you say you're working for again—and what do they do?"

"Department of Wilderness Management." He pointed to the badge, like we couldn't read. "We manage the wilderness."

"Uh-huh. And what are you doing?"

"Establishing a clear perimeter."

"Ah, with all due respect, sir—I'm not sure if that's a good idea." Harold sat back down. Making himself smaller. "We want them to leave, right? I'm trying to give them a good avenue of retreat. That's our plan—we'll keep them there until they get tired, feel like they've made their point, and go home." He hummed softly. "Does that, ah, not work for you?"

Todd removed his aviator sunglasses. “They are a group of heavily-armed domestic terrorists engaged in an unlawful activity—an assault on federal property. They need to be brought to justice. So, no, Sheriff Patches, I’m afraid that a ‘live and let live’ attitude toward enemies of the state does not *work* for me.” He popped the shades back on. “I’m taking charge of the situation. I’m looking for cooperation. If you’re not up for that, go home. Is that understood?”

“State property,” Bondurant said. “This is a state park. Not federal.”

Special Agent Todd turned his mirrored glare at Bondurant.

“And how’d you know about this anyway? I just got the call from Sheriff Patches. I don’t think he called you guys up.” Bondurant put on his grandfatherly smile. “Or maybe I’m just too old and confused to understand.”

For a while, the two of them faced off. Then Todd pressed his loafers in the gravel and walked away. “I’ll call if I need anything.”

Harold took off his hat. Crumpled it in his hands, staring at the gravel—a low and sad hum leaving his lips. “Arlo—maybe you ought to—ought to go back to my house. Check on Milo and the girls.” He had the brim bent, the fabric crumpling under thick squatch fingers. “I’ll handle things out here.”

A news van came rolling in next, dust and dead leaves dancing above the wheels. Exactly what he feared would happen—the story spreading and turning Nugget County into Wingnut Woodstock. I embraced Harold, giving him a nuzzle and a snort. Plenty of fear in his usual musk.

Our old home was turning into a battlefield—and it was my fault.

I made it back to the house and found Rosemary at the door, hands around her mouth—letting out a full-on bigfoot howl that echoed up the street. Families riding their bikes, walking their dogs, or doing lawn-work looked at her in horror, and so did I. Why was Rosemary howling, in panic and pain, at her Halloween decorations? I sprinted up to her, put my hands on her shoulders—saw the terror in her eyes.

“Milo.” She breathed his name. “He’s missing.”

“Where is he?” Was the cub in danger?

Then Harriet called from the living room. “Rosemary—I found this on the kitchen table.”

We hurried inside, Freshta waiting with her sniper rifle at the ready. All of us looked at the note, written on a post-it in Milo’s loopy handwriting.

Rosemary read it. “Dear Mom, sorry to scare you and I’ll be back soon, but I need to go and talk to Caitlin Candle about what’s happening and I think you probably wouldn't let me, so I'm sneaking out. I'm very sorry and I know I'll be grounded and probably lose a billion hours of screen time, but I think it's worth it. Caitlin's nice and her mom and dad are nice too. I'll explain to them that the wolves aren't dangerous, and they'll stop. I'll be back before dinner. Very, very, very sorry. Your son, Milo Patches." She looked from the note, the fear still there—but lessened a little now that she'd seen the truth. "He's going to the Candles."

"He writes a good letter," I said—though it sounded pathetic, given the circumstances. "Rosemary, you don't need to worry. I'll swing by Candlewick Ranch and pick him up. How about that?"

"Should I go with him?" Freshta asked Harriet—not me.

"Ah, better not, babe." Harriet hummed gently to Rosemary. "The Candle Girl's a schoolfriend of Milo's. He won't be in any danger."

"Right. You're right." Rosemary, convincing herself. "And Harold?"

I made like doe nuzzling her faun. "Just doing his job. Give him a call. He'd like that."

"I will. You bring my son back, Arlo."

"He's trying to fix things. To make them better," I said. "You can't blame him for that."

It was more than I was doing.

But Rosemary wouldn't be happy until Milo was back home. Especially with those stories Harold had told about families getting harassed. I gave her a final comforting grunt and went back to my pick-up. Was the news out? I switched it on as I drove over to Candlewick Ranch. And yeah, there it was. Domestic terrorists on some stations, freedom-loving patriots on others. Jerome and some of the other Rangers were taking interviews, all of them reciting Rusk's talking points. Asking for signatures to put Prop 33 on the ballot.

Rusk couldn't ask for better publicity. Back in the forest, animals would roar, flash their feathers, dance, or scent-mark their territory with urine to send a message. I have to say, Harrowers had them all beat.

I pulled into the long driveway of Candlewick Ranch. Sure enough, Milo's voice, clear and high, came from across the grass. I hopped the fence and loped over and there he was, standing at the foot of a tall oak with a treehouse wedged amongst the branches. His bike rested next to him, set casually in the grass, and Caitlin perched above the treehouse steps. They were talking amiably, Milo about to join her.

Then they spotted me and fell silent.

"Hey there, furball." I walked over and petted him. "Time to go—your mom's worried sick."

"Uncle Arlo, I just need—I need some more time." He looked back at Caitlin.

"You'll tell your dad, right? That wolves aren't dangerous? That they're such a great part of the environment, and that there are lots of ways to protect your goats?" A few of the goats wandered around, clopping grass, and watching us. "You'll tell him, right?"

Caitlin fidgeted on her seat. "He's, um, he's actually already got something to protect the goats." Then she glanced at me. "Maybe you should leave."

"Was just about do that." I rested my hand on Milo's shoulder. "Furball—come on."

"But we need to talk—we need to work something out." He was frustrated, sad, his bright eyes shining. "It's what my dad and mom were telling me, how bigfoot bands used to be. We'd share the woods. We have to share them now."

Then heavy hooves came dancing across the grass. I spun around. A strange creature came ambling toward us, accompanied by a few goats. A lean, shaggy monstrosity with four long, almost delicate hooves, ridiculous rabbit ears, and dark eyes below long lashes. An ungulate speckled brown and white, absurd in the fading Northern California sunlight, like something out of those books human children read—Dr. Seuss.

It let out a sort of burbling whinny as it sauntered forward.

I recognized the species, but what in the Holy Woods was it doing here? "Is that—"

"A llama," Milo explained.

"Oh no—Milo, Mr. Patches—you should get out of here!" Panic in Caitlin's voice. "That's Dolly! She's what'll protect the goats from the wolves."

Dolly reached us, placing one curious foot in front of the other and then stepping right next to me. I stared into her dewy eyes. "Seriously, she can't—"

Then Dolly's muzzle flexed. A blast of saliva walloped my face, sticky and stinking and clinging to my fur. I gagged, grunting.

"Okay." I wiped llama saliva from my face. "This is just—"

The llama reared up. Ready to attack.

Bigfeet were vegetarians—we were no threat to the goats—but Dolly didn't know that.

Quickly, I moved in front of Milo to protect him—just as Dolly's lean head lunged down and bit into my shoulder.

These were plant-eaters—their teeth were flat instead of sharp but having them settle on my arm for a hefty chomp still hurt like Hell. Dolly bit down, teeth crushing shirt, fur, and muscle. White-hot pain spread as I bellowed loud enough to make my throat raw. I tugged back, swinging blind—delivering a clumsy open-palmed smack to Dolly's face. She let go and I stumbled back as Milo and Caitlin screamed.

I could give this llama a bigfoot beat-down—but something told me that would do nothing to endear me to Caitlin's family.

Dolly's hooves came up next. Hurtling through the air, humming. A pair of lean sledgehammers aiming for my skull. I braced myself for it, darting back, raising my arms. Dolly was whinnying all the while. It sounded like laughter.

I was about to get worked over by a llama. The joke, after all, was on me.

Then another sound hit the air. Clear as a bell. A lilting, ululating chant.

The blows from the hooves never came. Dolly slammed her feet down in the grass.

I stepped back. Looked at Milo. He was the one making the noise, singing—mouth open, arms at his sides. As surprised as I was. Dolly was just staring at him. The same with the goats, some sitting on their haunches. Watching Milo like the cub was the Goat Grandfather reading them a story. He gasped suddenly, and his singing ended.

The goats went back to eating grass. Dolly joined them.

"What the hell?" Caitlin asked—the words absurd in her youthful voice.

I stared at Milo. "Furball—how'd you do that?"

"I've got no idea," he said.

"You know, I think I might."

Another voice from across the field. Candle's wife, hastening across the grass. Her dog bound alongside, barking excitedly. "Caitlin—oh my god!" She whistled and Dolly pranced back to her side, the goats trailing after her. "Milo Patches—what are you doing here? And you're—"

I spread my arms. Made the bite on my shoulder hurt even more. "Arlo Patches. Milo's uncle. I was here last night. I'm sorry about this."

She brushed pale hair behind her ear and looked at my bite. "Oh no—I'm so sorry. Oh my god—Dolly got at you. Here—come up to the patio. I'll get you an icepack." If she was upset about a bigfoot sneaking on her property, she didn't share it. "Milo, honey, why don't you come up too? And Caitlin, can you get some lemonade and cookies out?"

From being used as a chew toy by a llama to lemonade and cookies. Maybe my luck was changing.

A little while later, I was sitting on a wicker chair, munching on wonderfully soft chocolate chip cookies, and all was right with the world. Dinah—who had done some nursing before she married Ollie—had iced the growing bruise and even patched the rip in my shirt. Milo had a mass of crumbs in his fur, but he hadn't said much. Still waiting for the explanation of what he had done. The

Candles' dog, Bandit, noodled below him, eager for pets. While Dinah was away, grabbing me some pills, I told the kids what I could.

"When I was your age, furball, I heard legends about Singers—a special few of the Children of the Earth, who were chosen by the Forest." I sipped lemonade—just the right amount of tart. "They were supposed to be intermediaries between the wilderness and the rest of the world. Capable of talking to trees, to animals—to ask them to do what they wanted."

"Like magic?" Milo asked.

"Something like that. I never really believed in it, though I heard rumors of Singers up in Oregon and Washington. Always thought they were stories. You can't talk to coyotes and trees."

Caitlin looked in awe at Milo. "So, the Singers, they're like Santa Claus?" She went wise-beyond-her-years serious. "I know it's just my parents putting those presents under the tree."

"I don't know. What we just saw—that was real." I reached over and took Milo's hand. "Your mom and pop's got enough on their plate right now. We've got to tell them. I'm not sure when, but they deserve to know."

"I don't want to be Santa Claus," Milo said quietly. He was looking into Bandit's eyes. "I don't even know how I did it. The singing—it just sort of happened."

Dinah returned with some pills for me. I chased them with lemonade. Telling her that there'd been some bigfoot magic happening on her ranch was probably the wrong idea, so I changed the subject.

Not that this new topic was much better. "Dinah, I'm sorry about all this. Milo was trying to negotiate with your husband. Figure out some way to stop the occupation."

She sighed. "Jesus Christ, I'm trying to do the same thing. Ollie's gonna get himself in trouble—or somebody's gonna get hurt, all for the sake of this stunt. Even Ollie didn't really want to do it. It was that—that Eddie Jerome." She must have been watching her language with the kids around. "Do you know he's not even a farmer or a rancher? He works at the gas station." Maybe that had something to do with it. Why sell people gas and energy drinks when you could be a badass commando rebel?

"Speaking of which," I said. "Any idea where the new fancy-pants firearms are coming from? Some of them seem a tad more intense than what the Rangers usually carry."

"Sorry—when it comes to Ranger business, I stick to the bake sales." Her eyes went to Milo and Caitlin, who were now petting Bandit. The dog loved the attention, lying on his side to ensure that the tummy rubs kept coming. "Something to do with Jerome's new friend—that Rusk guy. I don't like it, Arlo.

I'm terrified that something bad will happen. I'm from Grizzly Hill, you know. When deals get made with dangerous people, it's always innocents who pay the price."

Bandit perked up, ears tenting. Squirming away from the kids and moving to the edge of the porch. He barked.

A car rumbled by. An SUV, working its way down the roundabout. The window rolled down and there was Wambach. Seated there like some big predatory reptile sunning himself on a stone. Looking out—watching us and saying nothing. He stared at Dinah, at me, at the kids. Then jabbed a finger out. Turning it into a gun. He pantomimed a few shots.

Was he aiming those at me? At Dinah? Or at Caitlin and Milo?

Either way, I was on my feet. A roar brewing in the back of my throat. Wambach hit the gas, twisted the wheel, and rolled out of the long driveway. He drove back to the main road. The message—whoever it was aimed at—clearly sent.

Stay in your lane or face the consequences.

I looked back at Dinah. "Do you have a gun?"

"A rifle, pistols—yeah. Ollie only took a few with him for his protest."

"Keep them close to hand. And if that guy, or anyone else suspicious comes by, you call the police right away."

"The police. Your brother." She reached over, taking Caitlin's hand. "They gonna be on my side?"

I lowered my eyes. I didn't have an answer.

I dropped Milo back off with Rosemary. She embraced him and escorted him inside—taking him straight to his room. She'd go easy on him. Milo took after his father and usually never got into trouble. It was kind of nice to know that he was following my example—just a little. I waved goodbye to them and pulled away. Grabbed some grub from a little veggie restaurant at the edge of town. A pair of massive tofu and barbecue sandwiches and a basket of onion rings. Some beer too. Settling cool in the base of my belly.

Gave me a chance to think.

Everything was spiraling out of control. The wolf picture was like a fuse, blowing up Nugget County. But who had set the charges? Me, for telling Kowalski to post it? That was true. But there was something else. I wouldn't even have seen that picture if it wasn't for Dr. Braithwaite. Stinko and Daisy had been hired to keep tabs on her by Rusk, and then he'd hired the Volk Vanguard to hunt them down after they failed. Braithwaite was the lure for all of us.

There was more about this case than any of us knew and she was the key.

Still in the forest.

I tossed the empty bottle and the crumpled sandwich wrappers to the passenger seat and drove away. Going for the state forest. That's where I'd find her.

I'd been distracted, thinking that I could play this the civilized way. Tailing people, asking questions, lying. The truth was that I needed to be an animal. A hunter. Sniffing out Dr. Braithwaite before the others could. Not that it would put a stop to this mess, but at least I could figure out how it started—and tell Walter Rose that I'd done the job.

Getting into the park would be tricky, especially now that it was turning into a standoff between cops and Jefferson Rangers. The main entrance—now swarming with Department of Wilderness Management agents—wouldn't work. I waited for the sun to go down, picked a stretch by a desolate country road, hopped the little fence, and went for a walk in the woods.

Cold now, with autumnal night making me put a windbreaker over my tattered shirt. I never needed one, back when I lived in the woods, but it lately seemed that everything had gotten colder.

Not much moonlight—a sliver up above, putting just a trace of pale light across the fallen leaves and pine needles. I started out, walking slow, conserving energy, pausing to rest a hand on the fuzzy sides of a massive redwood or on a moss-covered rock. This was where I'd grown up, and I'd often wandered in the dark. Traveling with the band in search of grub or—most often—sneaking away for a campsite raid. Bigfeet have big eyes. I could see decently in the dark, and better than that, I could smell.

A whole bouquet tickled my nose. Soil and the trees, rich and deep. Flowers here and there, adding a sweet spice. Animals too. A raccoon and her family who had been dumpster diving, perched on a branch up ahead and still stinking of trash. I gave them a glance as I pressed on. Trying to sniff out humans.

If I was Milo, maybe I could just talk to the raccoons. Ask them if they had seen anyone.

Instead, I had to do my own searching.I had to do my own searching. I reached a little stream running through a clearing and paused. Another smell. A tobacco tang—mixed with plenty of human body odor. Coming from just across the creek. I darted back. Made it to a tree and ducked behind it. A big redwood, thankfully, with the girth to hide my bulk. I crouched low, held my breath. Going quiet.

Just like in the old days.

Boots crunched on the grass and squelched in the mud. Flashlights winked in the woods. Four men emerged—and they weren't hikers. Long guns rested in their hands with flashlights slung under the barrels. Something told me they weren't hunters either—not a trace of orange on them. They didn't want to be seen. Dark camouflage outfits and watch caps. Bandoliers, powerful knives, high-powered weaponry—a scary combination.

Then there was the way they moved. Slowly and carefully, taking care with each step. They handled their guns in the same manner. No swagger like the Jefferson Rangers or carelessness like the Volk Vanguard. These guys were professionals.

A glance of a flashlight on a wrist revealed part of a spiky tattoo. I recognized it from some googling I'd done on Neo-Nazi symbols after tangling with Wambach. This looked like the bottom half of a Wolfsangel, another popular icon.

It represented, appropriately, a wolf trap.

I held my breath. These gunmen spread out a little, staring at the forest. One unzipped his trousers and took a whiz in the river. "Hey, Tugg." A broad-shouldered dude with an automatic shotgun slung over his back let out a whistle. "There's no one out here, man. Nothing but mule deer and trees. And what if those cops at the entrance start looking around? We should go back."

Tugg stood on a flattened stone, his back to me. He removed his knit cap, revealed a shaved head and skin the color of milk. "Wambach wants us to find the scientist."

"Wambach—we really trusting him? The Volk Vanguard are a bunch of clowns. You saw them. The Storm Battalion's meant for better things."

The Storm Battalion. They'd been in Wambach's file. Oregon-based group. Gunrunners, bank robbers, stone killers, with plenty of ex-military and hardcore criminals in their ranks—the real deal. Evidently, Wambach had invited them down for extra muscle. A sour bubble burst deep in my stomach. I couldn't even handle the Volk Vanguard without Freshta's help. These Storm Battalion dudes would catch me and skin me.

Slowly, Tugg stood. He walked over to Automatic Shotgun. Taking his time. Letting everyone breathe in the moment. "Are you saying I made a mistake?" He said it casually, with no menace at all, but I could see Shotgun flinch from where I stood. No doubt about it, Tugg was dangerous.

"No..."

"Because if you're saying I made a mistake, we can talk about it. We can reassess. Is that what you want to do? Right here in the woods? Have a little strategy session? Just you and me?"

"Tugg!" A call from a lean rifleman by the creek's edge. "Check it out. Footprints. Big one."

Oh, Burn the Forest. Those footprints were mine. And they were certainly big.

I'd lost my edge since the old forest days.

Tugg sprang over and looked at my print, clear under his flashlight and pressed deep in river mud. The flashlight shone out, illuminating my next print and the one after that. I clutched the tree. My heart was making like a raccoon scrabbling in a trash can. I took a step back, and another—moving to firmer soil. But it wouldn't matter. If I went fast, I'd rustle the underbrush and they'd hear me. I went slow and they'd catch me anyway.

And those heavy firearms would turn me into bigfoot salsa in a second.

I sucked in breath. Took another step backward, watching Tugg—tensing up, getting ready to run—and then something hummed over my shoulder.

Thudded into the underbrush further away.

The Storm Battalion spun around, aiming their rifles in the direction of the noise.

"Hey." A whisper to my right. I turned slow.

A woman, with dark skin below a set of night vision goggles, glasses on a chain dangling from her faded, dusty North Face jacket. She looked like she hadn't showered for weeks—and smelled like that too. "You want to live, come with me." A quirk of a smile. "Heh. Always wanted to say that."

I followed her, as the machinery in my mind cranked into overdrive.

"Sounds good, Dr. Braithwaite."

She crouched low and I followed her under those trees. Dr. Braithwaite moved with the same quiet as a mountain lion. She made me look loud. Made me look bad as well. I'd been hired to find her, to save her, and she'd gone ahead and done that for me.

Sometimes, the forest can be a real funny place.

LONE WOLVES

Dr. Braithwaite brought me back to her camp—actually *up* to her camp, since it was perched in the trees like a giant nest. She had arranged a set of boards around some projecting branches, and used it to house a tiny tent shelter, a little bedroll, and a host of telescopes, binoculars, and other scientific instruments. Only a redwood's spacious branches could accommodate something like that, and the whole camp creaked and listed to the side once I rappelled up, the branch making a moan and a pack of PowerBars dropped off and plopped to the forest floor.

"YOU WANT TO LIVE. COME WITH ME."

Dr. Braithwaite winced. "We gotta pick that up. Leave no trace."

"Appreciate that. I'm Arlo Patches, by the way. And I already know who you are." I scanned the forest floor, all in shadow now. "Storm Battalion won't come over here?"

"That's what those guys are called? The mercenaries?"

"Yup." I settled down. Barely enough room for the doc up here. I had wedged myself at the side, let my arm and one of my legs dangle down. "You're one popular scientist, Dr. Braithwaite."

"Biologist," she corrected. "And I'm aware." She counted on her fingers. "There were those two skunk apes. Then the big guy—and these goons. Now you." Braithwaite let out a low sigh. "And I've only got myself to blame."

"I wouldn't say that." I offered her my best smile. In the dark, it probably looked fit for Halloween—which was only a day away, if my memory served. "You're just doing your job. Trying to examine Northern California wildlife. You didn't know you were walking into a battlefield—"

"Except I should've." She unscrewed the cap on a canteen, staring into the distance. Her night vision goggles enlarged her eyes. Made her look like she was part insect—and a miserable insect at that. "Predators hunt in a lot of ways. Some chase down their prey. Others dangle a lure. That's what happened to me. I saw the lure—a famous creature, back in California at last—and went for it." A smirk. "I've studied snails. Waterfowl. Let me tell you, man—papers on slugs don't move units. But wolves? Everybody knows wolves. Top five charismatic megafauna."

Something didn't make sense. "You said lure. What do you mean by that? You wanted to see if there were wolves, right, and—"

"I knew there were wolves. Trail cams provided plenty of pictures. Some of them got radio collars too. Tells you wherever they go. Everyone knows, everyone's excited—and then I give a presentation at a private school in the bay and one of the kid's dads says that there's wolves running around his home, and I should come and do a formal report." Something wasn't adding up. I stifled a grunt and listened. "And, like an idiot, I come running."

One of the kid's dads. "That wouldn't be Walter Rose, would it?"

"Yeah." She looked somber.

"He told me you were going into the woods under your own steam. That you told his kid, and she got super excited, and when you disappeared, she got scared. Why I signed on in the first place." Holy Woods—the doc wasn't the only one who had been played for a sucker. "He lied to me. Lied to you too, it sounds like."

"I realized it soon enough. One look at this place, the ranchers and farmers close by, told me that if word of wolves got out, I'd ignite a firestorm." Which is exactly what had happened. "I tried to make a run for it, but his goons had staked out my car. Instead, I went into the woods." She hoisted up her canteen in a weak toast. "And I've been hiding ever since." She sagged on the platform. "No plan. No chance of escape. I'm a frightened animal. Trapped in the den."

"But you sent Kowalski the picture—"

She slurped from the canteen. "I didn't send him anything."

"But that means—"

"Rose got my computer and forced his way in. Found the pictures and sent them out from my account. Poor Kowalski's trusting enough to believe anything."

The revelation hit like a black bear's swinging paw. Rose had sent the picture. He meant me to find Kowalski, knowing that I'd convince him to release the snapshot. He knew I'd find Braithwaite later, to tie up loose ends.

He'd played me from the beginning.

But why would he want that? Why lure in Dr. Braithwaite at all?

Why did he want the world to know about wolves in the woods?

"It's all our fault, maybe." She pushed up the night vision goggles. Freckles against her skin and tired eyes. Reminded me of embers lost in the ash of fading fire. "Not your species, but mine. We never figured out how to share." Her arms went out, encompassing the woods. "Tourists. Locals. Animal lovers. Farmers and ranchers. Native peoples. Your species, Mr. Patches. All of us want the wild places in this world, and we need to figure out a way to share." Her eyes dipped. "But for some reason, learning to share is a feat that borders on the impossible. I don't know. Maybe the next generation will figure it out."

Made me think of Caitlin Candle and Maris Rose.

And Milo.

"So that's what you plan to do?" I asked. "Stay here? Wait for the next generation?"

Braithwaite leaned back, resting her spine against the vast tree trunk. "Why not? You can join me. Watch the wolves. Every so often, I catch a glimpse of one."

"No thanks. I need to see Walter Rose. Talk to him about what happened. Why he hired me—and you, apparently." I pointed down to the forest floor. "Want to come with me?"

"I think I'll be safer with the wolves."

I liked Dr. Braithwaite. Scientists and sasquatches had the same dry sense of humor. "I'll look after you. Got plenty of friends who can help." That seemed dubious. "My big bro's the sheriff. If Rose was up to no good, he can figure something out. Make sure these Nazi goons don't get you either."

"They're Nazis?" She closed her eyes, head pressed to the fuzz of the redwood bark. "Just wonderful."

"You'll be okay." I took out my phone.

"You got a signal with that thing?"

I checked it. "Nada, but we're in luck. There's a massive police encampment right outside the visitor center, not too far from here. The Storm Battalion boys won't dare to follow." She seemed intrigued—but still frightened. "Otherwise, you might as well put down roots here. What do you say?"

Dr. Braithwaite looked at her camp and closed her eyes. "I want to piss in a toilet again." She zipped up her windbreaker. "Let me do what I can to break camp and then we'll go. Leave no trace, remember?"

"Do what you can and come back for it later." I sniffed. "Dawn's not far off."

The last day of October. Halloween.

I helped Braithwaite collect what she could and stow it in an expansive backpack. Some of her camp had to stay behind, and she carefully marked the location in the GPS tracker dangling from a backpack. That would help us find the way out, though I wasn't worried. The first lights of dawn, a sickly gray, cut down through the boughs of the trees. And these were my woods. I knew them well. I may not be the sneaky squatch of my youth, but at least I wouldn't get lost.

That was the only relief we had.

The two of us started across, making our way through old deer trails in the direction of the visitor center. Now that the light was a little better, I could make out the same sort of trees, stones, and trickling creeks that had marked my childhood, pressed into my memory like a seam on folded paper. The world had seemed so much bigger in those days. A whole universe waiting to be explored in the broad limbs of a tree or an expanse of pine needle-draped soil. Then we'd made the decision to depart the woods, following the agreement of all the Children of the Earth, and I got to see how big the world really was.

Was it just seeing the old trees that made me a little sad? Maybe it was what anyone felt, bigfoot or otherwise, when they went home and thought about what it had been like when they were small—before they knew how hard things could get. In any case, the memories bit deep, and seeped their venom right under my fur.

Got me a little turned around too.

A strange smell added to the confusion. Dr. Braithwaite and I were hiking up a rise, making our way over a set of rough steps fashioned of stone and earth by some long-ago Civilian Conservation Corps workers, when the scent pawed up my nose and tickled my brain. I stopped. Dr. Braithwaite did too, but she couldn't smell it. Human noses were like human feet—they didn't realize how uselessly small they were. But I smelled it.

Wild on the wind. Rich and deep and with a threat hidden at the center. A sharpness of saliva and fang and tension in powerful limbs.

The scent of wolves.

"It's them, isn't it?" Dr. Braithwaite asked. "The pack?"

"There's a whole pack?"

"Yeah. Small family. I think one of their dens isn't far off." She continued up the steps. "Stay quiet. Maybe we'll catch a glimpse."

We kept going, staying low—making it up the staircase and to a little meadow.

Which went right to the back of the visitor's center, and its Free State of Jefferson flag.

I clenched my teeth. We hadn't gone around the Jefferson Rangers, like I'd planned. We'd come up right behind them.

"Hold on, man—hold on—give me a sec." A familiar voice. Eddie Jerome. He came walking from the center, a folding camp chair under one arm, a laptop under the other, and a phone pressed to his ear. I put a hand on the back of Braithwaite's windbreaker and stopped her, then slid a finger in front of my lips. Not that it mattered. We could have been a pair of Black Bears dancing a jig and Jerome wouldn't have noticed. "This is important. You can wait." He snapped open the laptop and rested the phone on his lap. "I'll put you on speaker."

A voice came over the phone. Sounded a little familiar. "You're putting me on speaker. Absolutely not."

"No worries. The other Rangers are still snoozing." Jerome clicked on the computer. "Gotta check my web store. Ah, hell yeah—merchandise is moving. Jefferson logo ball caps, Keep the Wolf from the Door t-shirts, my new Ranger Sweat small batch hot sauce—I tell you, if I'd known all you had to do to make this kind of money off merchandise was take over a state park, I would've done it years ago." He grinned. "What do you think, should I start selling a Jefferson Ranger baby onesie? Think that'd be a hit?"

Merchandising. Humans loved it—and that's what Jerome was doing. Riding the Ranger brand for all it was worth. I wasn't even surprised.

Dr. Braithwaite certainly was. She squinted at Jerome like she was examining some new and bizarre species. A self-proclaimed sagebrush rebel with a webstore. These guys were a conservationist's sworn enemies. To discover that one was considering marketing baby onesies had to be like finding a mountain lion in a multicolored clown wig.

The voice on the phone didn't sound impressed by small batch hot sauce and t-shirts. "We have bigger problems. What's the mood in the camp?"

Questions about the mood in camp—wait a minute. This guy was interrogating Jerome. And that's when I realized where I'd heard the voice before, even through the tinny static of the phone's speaker. It was Special Agent Rod Todd, the DOWM man who'd commandeered the entire standoff.

Jerome was a snitch.

It made perfect sense. Jerome had been the loudest voice in the room for the Rangers. Always urging them to get more radical, to take a bigger stand. He was the one who picked the fights, who seemed the most puffed up with their peculiar brand of patriotism and belligerence. The whole time, he was on the horn with DOWM. Taking marching orders from Special Agent Todd, while arranging for showdowns with law enforcement.

"The mood in the camp?" Jerome scratched the back of his neck. "I don't know. What do you want me to do, a survey?"

"If necessary."

"They're tired, I guess. Bored." He leaned back in the camp chair, trying his best to get comfortable. "A lot of the guys, they figure the point's been made. Everyone already knows about the dang ballot measure by now. And it's Halloween, isn't it?"

"I didn't notice."

"They want to go home. Take their kids Trick-Or-Treating. I'll be honest, I'm in the same boat. The Wi-Fi out here's miserable. I got, like, three podcast appearances lined up and I can't do any of them. Can barely check the store." He squinted at the screen. "Come on, Todd—can't we go home yet?"

"Have I said you could?"

"You've gotten what you wanted, haven't you?" Exasperation lending a panicked bleat to his voice.

"What do you know about what I want?" Todd's voice had the same imperiousness, the same coldness, that he'd demonstrated the moment he showed up. He was the kind of guy that gave commands, and everyone else had to fall in line. "Stay put. Another few days. Then we'll wrap it up. Think about it, Jerome—you'll have those podcasts salivating by the time you're done."

At first, the arrangement didn't make sense. Wouldn't Todd want the siege to end sooner? But then I realized what more time meant. More media attention. More chances for Todd to look like a hero. He wouldn't be the one stopping some small-time farmers who bumbled around a state park and went home a day later. Instead, he'd be a hero who stared down hardened domestic terrorists and won. As for Eddie Jerome, he boosted his profile big time. More guest star slots, more merchandise. More clout.

Everyone won.

Except for my brother, and the other Rangers, and the people of Nugget County.

And the wolves in the wilderness.

Next to me, Dr. Braithwaite frowned. I shook my head. We still had to keep quiet.

Jerome was on his feet, leaving the laptop on the chair. "And—and when it's done—when it's done, I'll be okay, right? The same with the guys? I mean, we'll pay trespassing fines—Mr. Rusk said he'll cover that—but nobody's looking at serious time. We haven't hurt anyone, right?"

No response from Special Agent Todd.

"It's not fair!" He sounded like Milo when the kid was younger. Throwing a tantrum.

"You don't like it? You shouldn't have gotten busted for credit card fraud."

"That was a big misunderstanding, man!" He circled the chair—and then a strange noise hit the air, a keening cry that echoed through the half-dark trees and distant hills. A noise that set little pricks of ice tiptoeing up your spine and added a tremor to your heart.

A wolf's howl. Close by.

Dr. Braithwaite gasped and stumbled back. The involuntary movement that humans did when a wild thing was close at hand. Jerome spun around, same panic in his face, as the crumpled wrapper of a PowerBar slipped from Braithwaite's pocket and floated in the crisp air. It landed gently the grass. A bright red ribbon, spaceship-shiny. Lying there on the grass. Jerome looked at it and then right at Dr. Braithwaite.

We could almost hear his thoughts, running on overdrive in the space of three seconds. How much had we overheard? Who else knew? What the hell was he doing to do?

"I'll call you back." He punched the phone. Then he reached for his belt, where a semiautomatic pistol dripping in expensive attachments rested.

"Wait just a minute, Jerome!" I leapt over the log, moving between the Ranger and the doc. "Think about what happens if you pull that trigger." He had it half-up, just about to clear holster. "The sound will echo over the State Park. My big bro and all the other cops will hear it, and they'll come running. Your friends are probably just waking up, still sleepy. One of them will panic and go for a gun and it'll be a bloodbath."

"We are not afraid to fight for our ideals," he snarled.

"Is that right? Then why were you just on the line to the Feds?"

Jerome's face went the kind of red that usually came from rashes. "No—you don't understand. *I'm* the one using him. We've got a relationship of mutual respect." He blinked his eyes. "Like Batman."

"Batman, huh?"

The wolves howled again. Jerome flinched. Getting caught in the act of snitching had done nothing good for his nerves and the wolves weren't helping. "Why are they doing that?" he demanded.

I knew the habits of some critters, but wolves eluded me. Not knowing what else to do, I looked at Dr. Braithwaite. "Their den must be close." She shrugged. "We're in their territory."

The back door to the visitor center creaked open. Four other men emerged, hurrying out. The wolf howls had stirred them—and they came armed as soon as they saw me and Dr. Braithwaite facing off with Ranger Jerome. Ollie Candle was with them, blinking sleep from his eyes and carrying a hunting rifle. The other Rangers were the same way, bleary-eyed, stumbling, weaponry awkward at their hips and Jefferson Ranger ball caps pressed down on hair tousled by sleeping bags. Braithwaite was shivering now, looking like she wanted to vanish inside her coat.

I'd promised to keep her safe. One of a thousand promises I'd gone and broken.

I kept my hands up. "Candle!" I raised my voice. "We don't want any trouble—we don't want to get you in trouble either. My friend and I will just slip around and get out of here." A flinty look in his eye. Call yourself a soldier and everyone else starts looking like an enemy. "Your wife, Dinah, your kid—they're worried about you."

"You visited my house?" Candle demanded.

A mistake. "Milo went there. Trying to reach you, to talk some sense into you." I took another step. "They're in danger. The people you're in business with—Wambach—"

"Keep your big feet right where they are!" He hoisted up the deer rifle. "What the hell are you talking about?"

"He was there. Wambach. He's Rusk's goon. That's your arms dealer, right?" I looked at the other Rangers and Jerome. "They know that? That you're in league with a pack of Neo-Nazis?"

"He's lying, man!" Jerome chimed in. Holy Woods—things were getting worse and worse. "Trying to divide us. You remember what he was like in the parking lot outside the school." He pointed, stammering—but I could tell his words were hitting home. "The bigfeet—they ain't like us. They're not people. And this wolf lady? An environmentalist freak. Let's throw them in the basement. Decide what to do with them later."

It was an imaginary line that humans—Harrowers—had invented.

Everything that was wilderness went on one side. Everything that was human on the other. For these Rangers, I was firmly on the side as the coyotes and the bears. Ragweed and locusts.

Candle flinched a little. It was a big step from civil disobedience to kidnapping. Besides, he knew my brother. He knew my nephew. Calling the kid 'not people'—he couldn't do that. Whether or not he believed me, the warnings about his family had scared him. After all, that was why they were there in the first place.

But before he could make his command, one of the Rangers pointed to the edge of the meadow. "Say." He was a big guy with a mountain man's bristly beard. "Is that—is that a dog?"

All of us looked at the edge of the clearing. An animal stood there. Certainly not a dog. The size of it was the first thing you noticed, a thickness in its limbs and in its rich gray pelt that no coyote and only a few domestic dogs could match. The color too, the shimmer of the gray and the silver, the brilliance of the cream-colored fur on the underside of its belly.

Then there were the eyes. Not yellow, not gold, but a dark, shadowy amber. They stared out at you from mottled fur, bright with intelligence that could never be caged or trapped. The wolf was everything wild, all in one package and standing on four legs at the edge of the grass.

Wasn't alone either. Another wolf, fur the color of a storm-cloud, popped up. Smaller pups behind them, trailing along. A little family. Mother, father, and kids.

The Rangers had called these creatures the enemy, but actually looking at them—staring at their beauty—made them more surprised than anything. Sure, they had talked about exterminating wolves, but seeing them outside a zoo or a nature documentary gave them the same kind of surprise that they'd get from seeing a dragon or a unicorn. They froze up.

It was the best chance we got.

I grabbed Braithwaite's hand. "Come on!" I pulled her along, breaking into a run. Charging through the ring of Rangers.

The spell was broken. The Rangers turned, shouting, and the wolves scampered away and vanished back down the slope. At least they'd be safe.

Which was more than you could say for us.

I made like a football player toward Beard Man. Rammed my arm into his gut and bowled him over, sending him into the grass and fallen leaves. Dr. Braithwaite scrambled after me, running for the boardwalk porch out back of the visitor center. No time to skirt it—and the house gave us more cover. We needed it, as a gunshot barked out behind us. A panicked shot, humming over my shoulders and cutting into the back of the house. Splinters flew and Candle shouted, ordering his men to hold their fire.

"No shooting, goddamn it! Capture them alive!"

He knew what would happen if the cops came in hard.

Dr. Braithwaite and I reached the door. Already open. We got inside, boots pounding after us. I glanced behind me—it was Jerome. We were witnesses to his betrayal. Candle could shout at him until he was hoarse. Jerome still wanted me and Braithwaite dead. He could explain away a lack of discipline—not a cozy relationship with the Feds.

I slammed the door behind us and locked it. That might buy us time.

"What do we do? What do we do?" Braithwaite panicked. Totally understandable.

I started across the visitor center's main floor. A little gift shop alcove hawking t-shirts and toy squirrels. Big exhibits on the local terrain, Indian artifacts, and wildlife. A large display featuring stuffed versions of the Charles E. Boles State Forest's residents: a coyote, bear, rattlesnake coiled up, and a plump beaver sitting on a chewed-up fake log and looking pleased at himself for being dead and taxidermized.

The Rangers had been sleeping in here, right across from the exhibit. We stepped on their sleeping bags and air mattresses. The door waited, right next to a collection of Modoc baskets and tools. Gray light through the wide window, the parking lot—and a little further, the police barricades. My brother would be there, surprised by the howling of wolves and the gunfire. If we could join him, we'd be safe.

If Jerome didn't gun us down first.

Or if the trigger-happy cops didn't shoot us as we emerged, thinking we were Rangers on the attack.

Another gunshot behind us, blasting apart the back door lock. It swung open. Jerome dashed in. Braithwaite screamed as he bumped into a stuffed deer, knocking it over. Jerome looked just as scared as us, but he hoisted up the pistol anyway. The Rangers were behind him, Candle still shouting out orders that he ignored.

I grabbed the stuffed beaver by its tail. Swung it around. Reminded me of a baseball player making a swing over the plate. The beaver lunged out and bashed into Jerome's face. Dusty fur and polished claws dug into his skin, and he stumbled, arms flailing. I brought the beaver up, clenched it with both hands, and drove it down again. Making like I was swinging a chair in a wrestling match on TV.

Jerome's legs dropped under him, and he plopped to the ground. Tried to bring up the gun, but I caught his fingers and squeezed. His bones were like a collection of twigs stuffed in sausages. A tension in my muscles, a grit of my teeth, and I forced them between the pressure of my grip and the unyielding metal of the handgun.

They broke. He wailed.

The pistol dropped and I kicked it away.

"Arlo!" Braithwaite shouted, pointing to the door.

More Rangers made it in, Candle leading them. Time to go.

I looked down at Jerome. "Maybe I'm not human," I said. "But I don't know what in the Holy Woods you are."

I ran after Braithwaite. She grabbed a bookshelf laden with hiking guides and history books and pulled. Volumes tumbled and the whole of the shelf crashed its way down, spilling books over the exhibits. Blocking the Rangers as they tried to cross their camp.

Then we crashed our way through the entrance and into the crisp morning air.

A run across the gravel and patchy grass. A dash toward the barricades. I had my hands up, hooting as loud as I could. A phalanx of assorted law enforcement officers waited—weaponry aimed over sawhorse barricades. Shouting out endless warnings at me and Dr. Braithwaite. A kaleidoscope of uniforms and guns and I was one bigfoot-sized target.

Dr. Braithwaite and I dropped to our knees, hands up.

"Stand down!" A familiar roar.

My brother.

Sheriff Harold Patches dashed in, hoisting up an arm. The deputies, Feds, Tribal Police—none of them fired. Harold looked down at me and sniffed. "Porcupine." He grunted as the various cops began to finally lower their guns. "What have you gotten into now?"

It would be one long explanation.

A little while later, Dr. Braithwaite sipped coffee from a Styrofoam cup, wrapped in a shiny thermal blanket, while I chatted with my big bro, Chief Bondurant, and Ranger Miller. They'd swept us away soon as we arrived, while the DOWM agents had their attention fixed on the visitor's center. The gunshots had spooked them, and they were gearing up for World War 3.

A picnic table council of war, away from the barricades and the chaos that had snowballed around the occupation. Besides DOWM, who had planted a hulking black sci-fi trailer at one end of the lot, a dozen news vans, and their crews were in full swing, already broadcasting what had just happened and piping in the details for their cadres of experts to dissect on National TV. To make things even kookier, some protestors and counter-protestors had shown up, each trying to drown out the other in an acoustic guitar showdown. About half of them were in Halloween costumes too.

Humans loved to make noise.

Harold looked defeated. His eyes had veins of red running through the darkness, his fur looked rumpled, and the upper three buttons of his uniform had long since been forgotten. Of course, I had missed a night's sleep too. Back in the forest, I'd be comfortable making a nice bed of branches and soft leaves and plopping down. Now, I wanted a bed.

But I had to tell them what I'd learned—once I made sure Special Agent Todd was out of earshot, giving an interview further down the trail.

Harold winced as I revealed that Todd and Jerome were connected. "He didn't tell us. Didn't tell us anything."

Bondurant, at least, didn't look surprised. "Confidential Informants have a long and illustrious career in law enforcement. Everyone's willing to make a deal—cops and criminals both. But this? Trying to make the Jefferson Rangers worse than they are? That's a little much. I think Mr. Rod Todd will be in hot water if it gets out."

"So why do it?" Miller asked. "Why risk it?"

"I don't know, man." Bondurant shrugged. "Book deal?"

But the reasoning didn't matter. We had to deal with the results, and what I'd overheard gave me some hope. "From what Jerome was saying, it seemed that the Rangers are nearing the end of their rope. They want this to end."

"Blaze of glory?" Miller asked.

I looked at Dr. Braithwaite. "Not once they know what I know. That they've been manipulated. Same with me. Same with the doc over there. Someone's been pulling all our strings."

Harold gave me a sniff. "You know who? And do you have evidence?"

I knew the answer to one of those questions. "Give me time." I stood. "I'll do a little more legwork. Show the Jefferson Rangers that they've been had. Once they realize what's going on, they'll toss down their guns and go home for Halloween candy." But was that wishful thinking? Bigfoot braggadocio? If I was after the truth, all of Rusk's hirelings—Wambach, the Storm Battalion, and Mr. Grey—would be running interference. "Trust me, Harold—I just need a little more time."

He looked back over the military standoff turned fall carnival breaking out in his jurisdiction. "I don't know how much more time I can give you."

Being asked to trust me meant climbing on weak branches.

"Arlo." Miller looked at me with sad eyes. "They might be manipulated, but they've trashed my visitor center. They turned a state park into something it shouldn't be. Don't forget that."

It was what Dr. Braithwaite had said. Humans needed to learn to share.

I gave him a nod, nuzzled my brother a final time, and headed off. Dr. Braithwaite slid out of the thermal blanket and trailed after me. I could have handed her over to the cops, but with Special Agent Todd not being an upstanding government agent, I had a feeling she'd be safer with me. My brother could keep Todd's G-Men underlings away. For now.

We walked back to the parking lot and a waiting deputy, who would give me a ride to my car. "I've got a place you can lay low," I told the doc. "Just, ah, be prepared to share it with two annoying skunk apes—but don't worry. You've seen them before."

She shrugged. I guess skunk apes made better roommates than hunters.

We cruised back to my duplex in the early afternoon, where Stinko's muscle car gleamed in my driveway. I'd spent the night running through the forest instead of sleeping. I needed rest, breakfast, and quiet—not to mention a safe place to stash the good doctor. The pulsating noises from my home told me that getting any of those things would be a challenge. I grunted loud enough to make the distant trees hear me and opened up.

Stinko and Daisy were shooting a music video. Ramon, my amiable neighbor, was filming them on his phone. Stinko had his shirt off, revealing the intricate swamp and gator designs shaved into his fur. Daisy danced next to him, matching the booming beat of one of Stinko's least listenable jams. She flashed a pump-action shotgun, and he held a gold inlaid pistol in one hand and—to make matters worse—Patterson in the other.

My cat, for his part, seemed to be enjoying the show.

They stopped their dancing as Braithwaite and I entered. The music kept going—repeating the words 'Gucci on a Gator, Balmain on a Bullfrog' in an autotuned croak, until Daisy reached over and switched it off. "Hi there, Arlo." She grinned. "We were wondering where you went."

I crossed the room, facing Stinko. He lowered the pistol and dropped Patterson. "Low profile." I snapped my teeth. "You understand what that means?"

"We didn't leave the house, bro. Door Dashed everything. I promise."

"And the car?"

"I peeled off the bumper stickers. It's completely unrecognizable." Holy

Woods. Stinko pointed to Ramon. "When we needed help to film the video, we texted him and he came on by."

Ramon gave me a weak wave. "What can I say? Their music's catchy."

"You see? Everything's totally safe." Stinko cocked his head at Dr. Braithwaite. "Hey, it's the wolf lady."

I grunted. "Wolf biologist. Doc? This is my neighbor, Ramon. And these two rock stars are Stinko and Daisy. They're the ones who were following you."

"Ah jeez," Daisy muttered. "We're sorry about that. If it makes any difference, we're the ones being hunted now."

"Yeah. We got tons of respect for you." Stinko reached for a Hawaiian shirt. "The way you hid from us? Masterful. And I love wolves. They're probably one of the coolest animals out there." Braithwaite smiled politely. "Inspiring too. You see, I follow an Alpha Wolf mindset and—"

"I'm sorry, Mr. Stinko—but there's no such thing as Alpha Wolves." Braithwaite settled into the kitchenette as I went to the fridge. Patterson hopped into her lap, and she smiled and gave him a pet—she liked cats as well as dogs, apparently. "I don't want to correct you or anything, and no hard feelings about you tailing me. I preferred you to those other guys, for sure."

I went to work on breakfast. Four EZ Veg Microwaved Breakfast Rolls, one after the other. Then a fifth, for Dr. Braithwaite. I shoveled steaming lumps of egg and veggie sausage into my mouth and washed them down with some Fireball whiskey that Stinko had left waiting on the counter. It burned its way down my belly, spice mixing with the heat of the breakfast rolls. Filling my gut with artificial fire.

Stinko accepted the bottle from me and gave it a sip himself. "No such thing as Alpha Wolves?" He sounded like a cub finding out the Guardian Tree wasn't real.

Braithwaite stared at the breakfast congealing on her plate. "Uh-huh. The research scientist who coined the term made a mistake. Thought he was seeing some wolf emperor and his underlings, when it was really a dad and his kids. He recanted, tried to get his old book pulled, but the term stuck. In reality, wolf packs are families. They look out for each other." She gave her steaming breakfast roll a tentative poke with her fork. "The whole hierarchy thing—that's my species. Not theirs. And not yours either, as far as I know."

Stinko tilted the bottle back. "Huh. You learn something new every day." He tossed it to Ramon, who managed not to spill any. "So what's the plan now, Arlo?"

I'd demolished the mass of food on my plate and settled back. Somewhat satisfied. I had more questions, more hunting to do—but I'd been up all night, twigs and dried leaves clung to my fur, and I had a feeling the real trouble hadn't even started yet.

"Now? I need to sleep." I pushed off from the table and drew out my phone. Set the alarm for an hour and a half from now—that's all I could spare. A little bit of oblivion, bringing me that much closer to Halloween night. "Don't play any more music."

"You got it." Stinko drew closer as Daisy went to help Braithwaite take some belongings out of her backpack. I'd let her shower before me and then she could take my bed while I passed out on the couch. "What the doctor said, about wolves looking out for each other. That's like me and you, right?"

"I spied on you and then you unloaded your stink glands into my face."

"Families fight sometimes." He hummed. "But you know that when it comes down to it, when you want help, you just have to ask."

I stared at Stinko. "Yeah, buddy. I know it."

"Hell yes." He clasped my hand and puttered over to Ramon for another snort of whiskey.

A little while later, I was lying on the couch, a couple gallons of Seaside Breeze shampoo worked into my fur. I put a pillow behind me. Patterson plopped on my belly. My eyes slid shut and I went to sleep.

Strange dreams.

A nighttime run through unfamiliar woods. A weird mix of the different forests that my band had visited in our youth. The redwoods of Nugget County stretched ahead, and then the trail twisted and it was the great sequoias further south, all dry and pale in summer heat. A collection of bones. Further on and I wandered through some full-on rain forest from way up north. Siskiyou or Umpqua, maybe. The sort of dense mist-shrouded land, with only thin lines of light cutting down on carpets of moss. More shades of green than you could imagine. So much green that it dazzled the eye, amazed you with how complex the Holy Woods could make the world.

But it wasn't paradise. I was being hunted.

Wolf howls cutting through the air. The same chill that I'd felt in the woods. Making my lungs swell with fearful breath. The almost silent step of padded feet on soft soil. The sort of fear you only got when wolves ran in the woods with you.

Except it wasn't wolves. I turned around and there were human forms with long guns. Hunters. No claws, no fangs, and they were still the masters of the forest. Compared to humanity, the Children of the Earth would always be second place.

I spun around, going back to the trail. Going to run—only to see Milo standing in the trail. He wasn't alone. A huge wolf on one side and Dolly the llama on the other. He was petting both.

MY EYES SLID SHUT AND I WENT TO SLEEP.

"Milo—" I started.

Then the wolf looked at me. "Balmain on a Bullfrog," he said, in the same electric voice as Stinko's latest DJ jam.

My alarm went off and I woke up. Late afternoon now. School would be out and soon enough, the sun would dip and add a mass of shadows to the leaf-strewn streets. Human kids—and their squatch counterparts—would go dashing from house to house in pursuit of candy. Back in the State Forest, some of their parents would be arming up, dreading the violence that would turn their Halloween night into a horror movie.

I didn't have nearly enough rest, but I had no choice. I had to go.

My house was quiet, at least. Daisy was on her computer, Patterson curled up at her feet. Stinko lay on the floor, headphones looking tiny on his huge head. Ramon had gone home, and Dr. Braithwaite still slept peacefully in my room.

I went to the cupboard and drew out an oversized bag of fun-sized candy. "In case we get any earlier Trick-Or-Treaters, you give them some of this." I dropped it in Daisy's lap. "You can handle that, I figure."

"I'll manage." She flashed me a smile. "I love me some Halloween."

"Oh yeah?"

"How often do humans give out stuff for free?"

I grinned back at her. For a pair of thieves, human Halloween traditions must be a delightful reversal. All you had to do was say the right words and folks handed over the goods. I headed for the door, pausing to button up my cowboy shirt and reach for my golf jacket. It was going to be a cold night.

"Where you going, Arlo?" Daisy asked.

I paused by the door. "Costume party," I said. "I'm gonna tear off some masks."

My pick-up waited. I got the engine going. Warren Zevon howling on the radio. Werewolves of London. How appropriate.

I started the drive to Terroir Valley.

Terroir Valley had gotten all gussied up for Halloween. Black and orange bunting strangled the streetlights. Oversized pumpkins loomed on the corners and shimmering bats hovered on lines strung overhead. It was still bright, but some electric decorations flashed to life anyway. Soon enough, Terroir Valley's wealthy tykes would be escorted amongst the ritzy houses, or maybe they'd just sit in their hefty homes on the hills for a Halloween party and let the spooky season come to them. Then the adults would come out, staining their costumes with booze as they partied the night away. Human traditions—they always seemed to be an excuse for people to do exactly what they wanted.

But who was I to talk? I gobbled human grub and drank human alcohol. I lived with humans, made my living off them too. And it was thanks to my stubborn need to try and be wild that I'd played right into human greed and nearly turned my home into a Halloween free fire zone.

Nothing spookier than that.

Once again, I drove up the winding road past the vineyards of the Rose Petal Winery. But the road to the huge manor house at the top of the hill had some new additions. Giant inflatable ghosts, Frankensteins, and witches flanked the road, pointing their way to the top. A small squad of zombies, frozen in mid-lurch, stood in front of a huge sign, glittering under Halloween lights. I squinted at it as I rolled up to the top.

Open Tonight—The House of Blood Red Roses. A New Vintage of Terror. All above a skeleton hand hoisting up a wine bottle.

A haunted house. Made sense. Walter Rose seemed like he had some ghosts in that huge mansion of his, skeletons hidden away.

I just needed to reveal them.

The gates were open—no need to give my name to the speaker. I pulled in, joining the long line of other cars—probably workmen and would-be ghouls taking a job at the haunted house—and went to the door. Would that stone-faced butler greet me?

Instead, it was Maris. Walter Rose's daughter was already in costume. Pale face paint, black lipstick, and a gothic vest. A black broad-brimmed hat with a black rose perched on the band completed the look. She gave me a nod and motioned for me to follow. "Um—hi. Everyone's out in the backyard, if you want to join them."

Everyone in the backyard? What was she talking about?

But I wanted to play along. I gave her a quick nod. "Sounds good. You'll have to be my guide, though. I grew up in the forest, but I could get lost in a place like this."

"Just follow me, Mr. Patches."

She led me into a vast parlor. We passed sheer walls the color of butter and tasteful, ultramodern light fixtures. Slim furnishings that looked as expensive as they were fragile. On the wall, framed awards for wine, for charity, for horsemanship, waited in neat rows. Some Halloween decorations too—monsters lurking in the corner.

Maris led me down a hallway in a sort of nervous half-step. "So, what, um, what are you supposed to be?"

"That's a question I ask myself every day. How about you?"

A little color crept into her cheeks below the face paint. "Vampire Cowgirl."

"Looks awesome."

She smiled at that. "I love your sister-in-law's costume too. It's so clever."

My sister-in-law? She was here? Fear crackled electric under my fur. I snorted, tried not to show it as something cold crawled around in my gut. This wasn't the sort of fear I'd felt in the dream—the fear of danger. This was worse. The terror that came when your family was in the firing line, when your actions had put them in the path of a forest fire and they would start cooking before you did. But I couldn't panic. Couldn't be afraid. Not if they needed me.

A large sliding door led out to a massive backyard, a sort of giant grassy ledge offering a perfect view of Nugget County. You could see the sprawl of vineyards, Sarsaparilla Springs, and the woods and mountains like a shadowy afterthought in the distance. Outside, Walter Rose had assembled picnic tables, a little gazebo, more Halloween decorations, a patio with a swimming pool—and most of my family.

I stood frozen in the doorway and took it all in.

Rosemary sat on one of the picnic tables, across from Walter Rose—both in costume. She was the Bride of Frankenstein, though as before, she didn't exactly understand the concept, wearing a huge plastic Frankenstein forehead below a bridal veil. Walter Rose was dressed as Dracula, the full Bela Lugosi, complete with a crimson ascot and slicked-back hair. He hoisted his glass as I stepped onto the patio, showing plastic fangs.

Harriet and Freshta sat at another table, listening in. Harriet's costume was a pair of cat ears, probably purchased in town. They didn't match her fur. Freshta, on the other hand, had a machete in a scabbard slung behind her leather jacket. It didn't look like a prop.

But all of my attention went to the middle of the lawn, where a game of cornhole waited. "Hey, Uncle Arlo!" It was Milo. He had a checkered, old-timey greatcoat, a clip-on bowtie, and a matching hat with flaps buttoned on the side. I recognized it a moment later.

Sherlock Holmes. The Great Detective.

Then a beanbag sailed easily through the air and dropped neatly into the goal.

Mr. Grey had thrown it. "Will you look at that, laddie?" He stood at the edge of the patio, wearing full highland regalia. A tartan kilt, a matching sash, and that humongous claymore dangling at his side. "Right braw toss, if I do say so myself. Now, why don't you give it a go?" He puckered his scarred lips at me. "Or perhaps your uncle wants to try?"

I walked onto the lawn, going next to Milo. "Sure thing, furball." Standing next to him and looking back at Mr. Grey as my heart pounded. A killer like that, right next to my nephew. The kid reached for the beanbag with the kind of heedless innocence you only got when you were young. What should I do? Roar at him and Rosemary to run? Pelt across the lawn and tackle Mr. Grey into the swimming pool?

No. That might tip my hand. Lead to my family getting hurt. "Thanks for looking after them, Walter." I kept my eyes on Mr. Grey as I said it.

"No problem." Rose was as oblivious as Milo. "Always good to get some extra guests at our haunted winery before we officially open our doors." He checked his watch—a very un-Dracula digital timepiece. "Ms. Patches? Hamilton should be here momentarily."

Hamilton Hamlin. Rose knew him?

Harriet shrugged. "That's okay. I don't mind waiting in a place so beautiful."

"Ah, Ms. Patches—you've certainly learned how to flatter."

That's what had lured them all here: Hamilton Hamlin. Rusk had mentioned something about Hamlin and HamCo—his father's company—wanting to get into environmental work. The pitch was obvious. *Swing by my buddy's massive Terroir Valley mansion. Bring the sister-in-law and your nephew. We're gearing up for Halloween. It will be fun.* Harriet had no idea that Rose was somehow responsible for this whole situation. And Rosemary? After the stress of her husband's job, getting herself and her cub out of the house and to somewhere safe must have been a gift from the Holy Woods.

"Did Hamlin invite you as well?" Rose asked.

"Yup," I lied. "Guess I was running a little late." Hearing all those names together made something click. I snapped out my phone as Milo wound up for a toss with the beanbag, Maris going to the other goal to prepare a throw of her own. I walked toward the gazebo, working my fingers against the phone.

Big and clumsy. I opened the wrong site—going back to Stinko's Stenchlife.com. Burn the Forest. A quick glance up at Mr. Grey, who was giving Milo some tips after Maris had scored a goal. He looked over my nephew's shoulder, staring at me—sparks of joy bright in his cold gray eyes. I glared back and went back to my phone. He'd pay for this.

There. Rusk's website. This time, I didn't go to the legalese or his list of clients. I went straight to social media instead.

I flicked through the pictures. Didn't take long to find the one I wanted.

Walter Rose, Lloyd Rusk, and Special Agent Rod Todd, all beaming around their plates at a high end restaurant. The sort of place where the waiters wore ties.

I read the description. Steaks With the Guys.

They were in it together.

Each one of them, pulling on a different thread. Lloyd Rusk wrangled the disgruntled farmers, turning their rage into headline-grabbing action and giving them the guns to make it stick. Special Agent Todd kept the Rangers on a short leash, thanks to his confidential informant. He'd handle law enforcement too—as well as my brother.

And Rose? He started it all. Played Mr. Nice Guy Nature Lover and got Dr. Braithwaite to head into the forest, to make the appearance of wolves official. And when she didn't want to play ball, he'd gone ahead and hired me.

I'd done exactly what he wanted. We all had.

And I'd bet both my fangs that once it was all done, Rusk's criminal connections through Mr. Grey—Wambach and his Nazi pals—would eliminate every link. Braithwaite. Stinko and Daisy. Me.

My family.

Only one question left. Why? Why divide Nugget County against itself—not that they had to work so hard to do that—and risk a world of legal action from gunrunning, corrupt cop shenanigans, and murder? Humans had such a deep capacity for hurting the world around them, but they rarely did it for no reason.

I needed to know. And I needed evidence.

I slid the phone down, forcing the thoughts away. Mr. Grey stood there, right in front of me. Watching. "Your nephew, Arlo." He pointed to the kid, who was now hoisting up his beanbag—trying to help Maris sink in her shot. "He's a good sort. Though I don't quite understand his costume."

"He's Sherlock Holmes." Rosemary approached, holding out a glass of wine for me. It looked dinky in her large hands. "You know, the detective." She winked at me. "In honor of you, Arlo."

"I'm the one who's honored," I said. "Are you staying here all day, Rosemary?" Keeping my tone calm. A waste of time, maybe. Mr. Grey knew that I knew that something was up, that we were both playing pretend.

"Until it gets darker. I think we'll check out the haunted house, then take Milo home. He'll want to go Trick-Or-Treating with some friends." She looked at Milo, who was preparing to toss his own beanbag. "Don't worry. I'll hang back. Don't want to embarrass you."

"Mom!" Milo called out—clearly embarrassed anyway.

So they'd be here—in the firing line—for the foreseeable future. I shifted a little, considering what to do. Rose—I needed to get him alone. Make him see what happened when you pissed off bigfoot. That would be my family's ticket to safety. "Well, while we're waiting." I drained the wine glass. Added it to the alcohol already simmering in my belly. "Walter—would you like an update on the case?"

Maris looked up. "Dr. Braithwaite?" Real concern in her voice.

"Why don't you stay out here, honey?" Rose left his chair, his vampire cape rustling. He patted her shoulder as he walked over to join me. "We'll talk in my study."

She looked like he'd asked her to swan dive off the veranda.

Going with Rose meant leaving my family outside with Mr. Grey. Would he really try anything in the fading fall daylight with Maris Rose sitting there and watching? Probably a bad idea to start swinging a sword with the boss's daughter close by. And there was Freshta. I hadn't seen Mr. Grey in action, but he seemed fearsome. Freshta, though—she was a soldier. If anyone could give him a run for his money, she could.

Still, it hurt to go. I walked over to Milo as he wound up for another toss. "I'll see you soon, furball. And I love the costume. Let me know if you solve any mysteries."

"Okay," he said—like that was no problem at all.

The detective business—the stories always made it seem so easy.

JUDAS GOAT

I followed Walter Rose deeper into his cavernous home. He was yammering on, a bird singing away to nobody. "I always pull out all the stops around Halloween. One of my favorite holidays, for sure—I love monsters and mayhem. Love to be scared. And it's for Maris too. Her mom's in the Bay, always treats her to the best of everything, so when she's staying with me, I've got to make it special."

He led me into a spacious chamber ending in a wall-sized window that let us look down at the vineyards, the haunted house, and the grounds. Like a king's balcony in a castle. Neon pumpkins flared to life, glowing orange eyes watching the road. It looked like he'd made a full-on gothic graveyard, complete with mist, just below the haunted house and next to the stables.

"But let me tell you, Mr. Patches—this kind of Spooktacular doesn't come cheap."

"I'll bet," I said. "Mr. Rose, I need to know what—"

But then the door opened behind us and Maris stormed inside. The vampire cowgirl beat me to the punch.

"Where's Dr. Brathwaite, daddy?" Her eyes went to me, flashing after the last word. "You're hiding something. I know you are."

"What are you talking about, honey?" Rose put on an ingratiating smile, showing off his plastic fangs. "I don't know where she is anymore than you do. That's what Mr. Patches and I were about to discuss."

I stepped back, hands in the pockets of my coat. When Dracula and Dracula's daughter started arguing, it was best to steer clear—and listen.

"I know why she ran. She was scared. She found out what you were doing." Maris advanced on him. "I've been listening to the news. We talk about it at school. The wolves. The occupation. The bill—what's it called?"

"Prop 33," I jumped in.

"That's it. You and Hamilton Hamlin and that Rusk creep were talking about it." Another step, her shining black cowgirl boots—with little silver skulls on the toes—drumming toward him. Rose fell back until he bumped up against the huge window. Trapped. "I know you're in debt. I know you keep spending money. And getting the government to give you tons of cash for some sort of development thingy in the woods will solve a lot of your problems."

He faced me and chuckled—a plump raccoon trapped in a dumpster. "Teenagers. What can I say? Arlo, maybe you'd better step outside and—"

Then Maris's eyes narrowed, and she went in for the kill. "Mom's right about you."

His smile stayed, his eyes going crinkly and sad. "You don't know what you're talking about."

"I didn't believe her." Her voice went up. High and angry. "But I do now."

"Oh, what the hell does she know?" Rose's voice rose to match his daughter's, the plastic teeth tumbling from his jaws. He hoisted up a hand, swirling his cape. "What's she ever done, besides arrange five-hour brunches and get sloshed on Bloody Marys? I'm the breadwinner. Always have been. I'm sorry if the way I make a living's not up to your exacting moral standards, Miss Maris—"

"You used me to get to Dr. Braithwaite!" She shrieked back. "You knew I care about animals—about wolves—and you asked me to introduce you to her and then you—you sent her to the woods and then the news spread and—"

"I never made anyone do anything they didn't want to do!" He roared out the words. Trying to convince Maris—or himself? "Dr. Braithwaite's got a budget. Just like me. She wants to publish papers, textbooks with her name in the by-line, a cushy tenured job at Stanford or Berkley. I mention wolves in California, she sees dollar signs." Now, the momentum was on his side. Maris stared at him, unable to think of a comeback. "You're thirteen. You think the world works the way it does in movies. What do you think pays for this place, for your private schools, for the donations you get me to send to save the wolves, the whales, the sea otters—for the goddamn alimony? Yes, Maris, I'm in debt, and I'll do anything I can to get out. For your sake."

She took off her goth cowgirl hat and crumpled it in her hands.

"You worried about the ranchers? The farmers? Bunch of hicks. Should've learned a long time ago that we're in the age of the knowledge economy. They can get new jobs. Maybe in the new developments that I'll put up in this area. Cheap housing. Easy commutes. It's what we need."

"They're picking a fight with the police!"

"They're big boys—they can live with the consequences of their actions. And if they get busted and have to sell their ranches for their legal fees, I'll be right there with sweet deals, ready to put the land to better use. We're in a housing crisis, Maris. Do you get that?"

Maris's voice was quiet. "What about—what about the wolves?"

"They can go back to Oregon. They'll be safer there."

I took my hand out of my pocket. Revealed the little tape recorder—a PI classic—that I'd kept there. I'd been recording the whole conversation. I clicked it off. That noise—terrible as a predator snapping their jaws—got Rose's attention away from his daughter and to me.

"And I was just another little prop for your display," I said. "The Rangers, the wolves, Dr. Braithwaite—and me. A nice little all-American tableau you can put in your front yard to attract the Trick-R-Treats while you keep all the candy. Am I wrong?"

His fingers curled around the plastic fangs. "What are you doing, Patches? With that recording?"

"You're asking if I'm gonna blackmail you? I don't know, Rose. What would you do?"

"You've got to do it, Mr. Patches." Maris looked from me to her pop. "Get him to stop this. Leave the wolves and the ranchers alone and—"

"Maris—honey—shut up." And she did. Rose sucked in air. Arranged his face into something conciliatory—a reasonable businessman. The vampire get-up kind of ruined it. "You've got to ask yourself, Mr. Patches—what will happen if that recording gets out? You think I'll be arrested? I haven't broken any laws. Neither have my friends."

"Manipulating a CI to start a domestic terror incident." I brought up Special Agent Rod Todd. "DOWM usually frowns on that sort of thing, if it gets out. And you're part of the same little club, ain't you? Steaks with the guys?"

He smoothed back his slick Dracula hairdo. "How long have your people been out of the forest? Living with us? You think by now you'd have figured out the way the world works. There was no coercion. Jerome and the Rangers acted on their volition. Same as everyone else in their little drama."

He was right. Todd was the Special Agent, Jerome was the snitch—could a DOWM Man really go down for pulling Jerome's strings? Jerome had wanted it too—eager to rocket to notoriety and trade that for clout and cash. This was how humans like Rose, Rusk, and Todd hunted. They didn't go stumbling through the woods with rifles. Instead, they lay bait and waited.

Jerome, Braithwaite, and me—we'd all gone for the bait and gobbled it up.

Except that it was poison. Rose got to keep his hands clean, and we died anyway.

Rose seemed to realize that I was beaten. Maris too. Her eyes lowered, her shoulders slumping. The gothic cowgirl get-up made it look even more tragic.

"And there's something else you should've realized, Patches." Rose put his hands on his daughter's shoulder, pulling her to the side. "Something you forgot about your own kind."

"What's that?"

"Just how quiet they can be."

A gentle click of metal. A brush of fabric.

I spun around. Mr. Grey stood there, in all his tartan glory.

"Happy Halloween." He smiled, showing off his cut-cheek smile—and then he punched me.

The kind of powerful blow that only a bigfoot—or a Fiar Liath's—fist could deliver.

The bomb went off in the middle of my face. I tumbled back, forgetting how to stand as the world went runny and blurred. Orange and black, melting together. Halloween swirl. Another blow, this time to my belly. More followed, rapid blows to my gut and ribs. I managed to put my hands up, block a few—but the fight was his. We both knew it. Mr. Grey was stronger than me, and faster too. Not to mention bigger. Every animal in the forest knows that there's fiercer predator, waiting for the right time to pounce. Now, I'd found mine.

From somewhere far away, Maris screamed.

I crashed onto the hard wood floor. Then Mr. Grey was on top of me, an endless pressure in my belly as fuzzy hands settled around my throat. Was he gonna strangle me? Snap my neck? Or just pick up my head and bring it down against the polished hardwood floor until my skull cracked and painted the floor with my brains?

I was too far away to care.

"Grey!" Rose's voice. "Not here—for Christ's sake. Not in front of my kid."

"Oh, I wouldn't dream of it." Mr. Grey's fist went up. A distant silver comet. "He's coming with me."

"Where are you—never mind—I don't want to know."

Maris sobbed. "Daddy—he's just—how can you—"

"He'll be okay. Mr. Grey's just gonna give him a talking-to. Teach him not to try and blackmail anyone." He pulled back my fingers. Drew out the recorder.

My one bit of leverage—already gone. "You'll see him again." Rose must be used to lying to his daughter. "Keep him away from the haunted house, okay?"

Something tugged at my arms. I slid across the floor. "Something tells me that's not the proper scare you're after. Don't worry." Mr. Grey loomed over me. Showing off that scar-faced smile again. "We'll be Trick-Or-Treating somewhere else."

His head slammed down. Gave me an up-close look at those scars—a pair of twin pale snakes coiling through his facial fur—and then he rammed the dome of his heavy skull against mine and sent me straight into dreamland.

I drifted in and out as we rumbled through Nugget County, back to Sarsaparilla Springs. Lying in the backseat of a hulking Range Rover, catching glimpses of Halloween light and night sky through the tinted window. My wrists ached. Felt like foxes had been nibbling on them. I twisted my neck, looked down, and saw why—plastic zip ties. Mr. Grey had fixed a pair on my wrists, fusing my hands together in front of my belly. They were strong and doubled-up too. Nothing on my legs at least.

But that meant he wasn't going to give me time to run.

By then, things were starting to make more sense. I breathed in and out. Crusted blood on my fur, giving me a rusty moustache. Ribs had been worked over too. Didn't feel like anything was broken, but that was about the only relief. I squinted through the windows. Darkness outside the glass. No houselights. No Halloween decorations.

We were cruising through the woods.

Music booming on the radio. Peppy 80s beat. Booming vocals.

Duran Duran. Hungry Like the Wolf.

"Doo-doo-doo-duh-doo-doo-duh—" Mr. Grey was singing along until his cell phone buzzed. He snatched it up. "Hello there!" The other voice was a static crackle. "Ah yes. I'm nearly there. Should get there just about the same time as your Aryan brothers and sisters ring the doorbell." Wambach. He was talking to Wambach. "But I gotta ask you, do you really think the Vanguard can handle the job?" What job was he talking about? "I know. It's nothing but a housewife and a little girl. But the point stands."

A housewife and a little girl. Dinah and Caitlin Candle. We were driving through the woods, heading to Candlewick Ranch. It seemed like the Volk Vanguard were already on their way.

I wanted to groan. To howl. To roar. Instead, I said nothing. Played possum.

But it all made sense. Ollie Candle was a link between Rose, Todd, and Rusk. He had to be cut. His family too.

But why bring me to the murder scene?

And then I realized it.

What would make the Jefferson Rangers even more determined to make war on nature? A bigfoot gone mad. Wiping out one of their families. I'd die in the attempt, of course. A berserker bigfoot, succumbing to his wounds after killing Dinah and Caitlin Candle. Maybe they'd finish Ollie off later—or maybe he'd be so maddened with grief he wouldn't think to question the story. Todd could finesse everything—and there'd be no witnesses.

Now, I really wanted to roar.

Mr. Grey sighed. "All right, all right. And a final question—do we have to deal with the child as well? I can make sure she sees nothing that'll contradict the—" More arguments. "Okay. You've made your point clear. I'm pulling in now—yes, I'll call you when it's done."

But Wambach wasn't shutting up.

"Oh, Mr. Rose? Did Rusk give that order or—" Mr. Grey chuckled. "Ah. Well—won't he be surprised?" What did that mean? Was there trouble between the trio? The Steaks With The Guys Squad turning against each other? Or was Wambach deciding to play executioner himself? "Right. Have yourself a Happy Halloween now." Mr. Grey switched off the phone.

Back to the radio. Hungry Like the Wolf reaching its chorus before ending abruptly as he killed the engine and parked.

He looked back at me. "Did you catch any of that?" He knew I was awake. Burn the Woods. Another card out of my hand. "Here's a little Halloween treat. Make sure you won't tell anyone." He lunged back, a candy apple glistening with caramel in his hands. He slammed it in my mouth, gagging me. Cloying caramel apple stung my tongue. Now I couldn't scream if I wanted to.

He opened the door. Moonlight and cold air as he grabbed my legs and pulled me out. I slid over the seat and plopped onto the dirt. Patchy grass. Dark loam.

I tilted my head to the side. A fence, the arched entry to the ranch. Shapes in the darkness.

The goats. And something else.

Maybe I had a chance after all.

Mr. Grey stretched his arms, limbering up. "I'm not in the habit of wasting time. I'll be taking your head. We'll say that Mr. Candle done it to you with a hatchet after you ate his wife and little one. Then, he shot himself out of grief."

I grunted around the candy apple.

"I know, I know—we don't eat meat. But that's how they see us, isn't it?" He pulled the claymore out of the passenger seat. It caught moonlight. Made the big blade shine like a lightsaber. Behind him, casually crossing the grass—a lean shape. Dolly the llama, coming to save me. Come on, you beautiful llama. Come on. "We're nothing but monsters. The scary stories around the campfire. You might as well make some money to play the part."

Then he pulled back his sword.

Hooves pounded in the dirt. Mr. Grey paused. Looking up. Didn't even have time to unleash a storm of Scottish swears before a llama's lean face jabbed into his shoulder and bit down. He gasped, grunted, roared—tried to bring up the sword and caught a pair of flailing hooves to the upper chest. Dolly sent him stumbling back as she landed hit after hit.

He dropped the sword.

I scrambled for it. Crawled over the grass, dragging my jeans against the grass. The claymore had fallen on its side. I gripped the blade, cut my finger on the edge, and tilted it on its side. Then pushed the plastic zip-ties against the metal and worked them back and forth.

"Mad beast!" Mr. Grey managed to land a blow on Dolly—and sent her sprawling. The guard llama was plenty powerful, but Mr. Grey had one hell of a right hook. She made a raspy hiss, unloaded a blast of spittle in his face, and galloped back to the house.

Just as a gunshot thundered through the air.

The Volk Vanguard. They must have shown up.

I didn't have much time.

The plastic frayed. I kept working on it as Mr. Grey advanced. Gritted my teeth. My heart pounded. Fur stood on end. He reached me, fist stretching out. Getting worked over by a llama had made him angrier than usual.

The plastic snapped.

I wrenched out the apple with one hand, turning it into a sugary comet, and grabbed the claymore with the other. I brought up the sword, swinging it as hard as I could at Mr. Grey. It cut through the air, humming. More gunfire coming from the house. Dinah must be trying to hold out, to fight off the Volk Vanguard—defending her daughter. Human and bigfoot mothers have a lot in common. I needed to help her. Needed to end this fast. Another stab, another slash. Mr. Grey moved back, going toward his car. He backed into it.

"Arlo—"

I lunged out with the claymore. A clumsy stab—closest I've come to a sword was a stick in the forest—but it rammed through his hand, cut deep, and kept going. Plunged straight into the upholstery of the Range Rover's back seat. Punching through flesh, muscle, cushion, and deep into the interior of the car. Pinning him down.

Mr. Grey wailed. He had a big hand, but the claymore was a big blade. Bigfoot strength had got it through a good portion of flesh and the car door. Fat drops of blood—black in the night—welled up and ran down onto Mr. Grey's kilt and the car seat. He wasn't going anywhere—but he wasn't out of commission. I tugged at the blade and it didn't budge. It would take more time to pull the sword free and finish him.

Time that the Candles didn't have.

I punched Mr. Grey—a nice return for what he'd given me. "Don't go anywhere." The blow sent spittle and more blood onto the car door and the grass. He collapsed across the seat, and I punched him again.

Then I spun around and ran for the ranch house.

I hopped the fence. Saw them, lined up behind an old station wagon. Using the car as cover as they aimed an assortment of firearms at the Candle house. Brenda Stull led them, now dressed in hunting cameo and a shockingly pink headband—one bit of frippery. She fired a pump-action shotgun from the hip, blasting apart a window. Guess they figured they could gun down the Candles and make it look like a bigfoot attack later. Three Volk Vanguard goons backed her up—and they spotted me coming down the driveway.

I'd forgotten to be quiet.

Stull spun around and racked her shotgun. "Well, well." She grinned savagely.

"Patches!" Dinah Candle shouted from the house. A dog barked. "In here!"

I'd come to save them, and she was saving me.

Candle's rifle fired away—rapid shots, booming against the Halloween night. I ran for the door, slipping on pine needles and fall leaves. Stumbling, weak, ducking as Stull's shotgun roared again. The shell punched through the air above me, making the night hot.

I reached the door. Candle slammed it open, then slid back so only her rifle's muzzle poked out. It roared again as I jumped inside and sprawled on the mudroom floor.

"You okay, Arlo?" Dinah slammed the door shut behind me. She had one of those modern lever-action guns, cartridges stuffed in the pockets of her mom jeans. She worked the lever and ducked back as more bullets punched through the door. Splinters flew, white and dancing. I low-crawled around the corner and joined her. A shot whined over my head and took out the mounted deer's head. Sent stuffing and antlers flying.

I rolled over, sat hard on my bottom. "I'm just glad you guys are okay. Is Caitlin—"

"In the kitchen." Dinah motioned for me to follow. She wore a bright orange fuzzy sweater with a grinning Jack-O-Lantern on it. "You good to shoot?"

"YOU GOOD TO SHOOT?"

"Yes, ma'am." I hustled after her.

The kitchen offered slatted windows, looking out at the front of the ranch. Caitlin—wearing a unicorn onesie—huddled behind the kitchen island, hugging Bandit close. He had a costume too—a stripey prisoner shirt. I tried to put a comforting smile on my face and give that to Caitlin, though my bloodied, leaf-strewn fur probably didn't help. She smiled back.

Their defenses weren't much. A single bolt-action rifle sat on the counter. You couldn't win a gunfight with a slow-firing gun like that, but I didn't have a choice. I scooped it up.

Dinah and I worked our weapons in tandem. The clear, high crack, an animal's warning cry, and the familiar pressure against my shoulder. All familiar as my own fur. I hadn't pulled a trigger in months, but the memory never really went away. I hit the window of the Vanguard's station wagon, showering them with shattered glass.

We ducked down together too. "You called for help?" I asked. "The police?"

"Yeah—they promised help—but I don't know—"

I grunted. All the cops in town would be occupied with the occupation, and Halloween was always a bad night for law enforcement anyway. Dinah seemed to realize the same thing. Her eyes tensed, going to Caitlin—full of fear. "I called Ollie too." More gunfire from the Volk Vanguard. Rapid blasts of unaimed thunder. They tore apart the window. Sundered the blinds. Bandit barked and Caitlin screamed. "Do you think—do you think they'll get here in time?"

"Sure," I lied, but I reached for my phone too.

I knew somebody closer.

I hated to do it. Hated to ask for help, hated to risk putting my life in a pair of shaky, stinky hands—but Dinah and Caitlin needed help, and I owed them. They were in the same trap as me, and I was one of the people who had put them there.

I sent a text message to Stinko. The request for help. The address. About a thousand exclamation marks. Then I hit send.

When it was done, I looked back at Dinah. She slid more rounds into her rifle, thumbing them in with trained precision. "I'm sorry about this," I muttered. "Sorry about this whole goddamn mess. For whatever that's worth."

"It's not your fault. These are the boys Ollie was playing with—same with the guy who drove by last time you were here." Dinah clicked the lever into place. "I was all set to take Caitlin into town for some Trick-Or-Treating. Halloween's ruined." She grimaced. "Ollie's got a lot to answer for."

"It ain't all his fault," I offered. "Your husband's been manipulated. Same as me." And Dr. Braithwaite. And my big brother. "As a matter of fact, I think the only two people in this town who were clear-headed and sensible about this thing are your daughter and my nephew." Maris Rose too.

"So what do we do now?" She clutched the rifle, but I held up a hand.

The Nazi contingent slowed their barrage. What were they doing? Planning some sneaky flanking maneuver or gearing up for a big-time blitzkrieg through the front door? I shuffled my way around the kitchen island. Staying low, careful to avoid chunks of shattered glass and splinters from the blinds, along with the ceramic remains of a big cookie jar. I reached the wall, rested my back on it.

Raised my voice to a bigfoot shout. "Stull?" I shouted her.

"Is that you, Arlo?" Stull replied, still cheery. "Save your breath. We got nothing to talk about."

"How about the fact that the police are on their way?" Maybe the Volk Vanguard would spook easy. "My brother doesn't like Neo-Nazis raising hell on Halloween. You want to surrender, talk about who sent you, it'll go better for you."

"We don't have to worry about the law."

Why not? Well, if they were Wambach's goons, then they were part of the conspiracy. Maybe Wambach and Todd had some arrangement. Explained how Wambach avoided serious time while committing serious crimes.

I looked at Dinah, who was as scared as I felt. In the Westerns, everyone knew what happened if the cavalry didn't arrive in time.

Then one of the Vanguard, Stanley, the dude who liked pontificating about Hitler's love affair with the yeti, let out a terrified screech. "What the hell is—"

That whickering hee-haw hit the air, followed by a meaty thump and a sudden scream.

Dolly to the rescue.

More shouts, screams—shattering glass. Dolly was earning her keep.

"Mom." Caitlin looked up from where she crouched. "Mom, they'll kill her." And she was right. Dolly could do some real damage, but the Volk Vanguard would put a bullet in her in a second and even a superpowered guard llama couldn't survive that.

Dinah just shook her head. Nobody was dumb enough to go out there.

Except me.

"Cover me from the door." I stood, clutching the rifle. "I'll get the llama."

It was pure idiocy. The house offered cover, plenty of ammunition, and a chance to hold out until help arrived—and I didn't even like that llama. But Dolly didn't deserve this, any more than Dinah and Caitlin.

So I ran to the door, shoved it open, and then I was running across the driveway, going to back up a llama in an attack against Stull's Nazi hit squad.

I neared the car. Stanley, his face bleeding, had shoved Dolly back and aimed a nasty long-barreled revolver in her direction. Her huge eyes with their absurdly long lashes gleamed in the moonlight. I couldn't let that llama die.

I ran for the car. Jumped up and landed on the hood. Metal crunched. My knees ached.

I kicked Stanley full in the face.

He flew, arms flailing and pistol dropping as he made like a reverse superman and crashed into the waiting fence. The third, pimply Pomeroy from the casino, tried to help him and caught a llama hoof to the jaw—but then Stull was aiming the shotgun at me, racking the pump to fire. I hurled myself down from the hood of the car. Dropped onto the dirt. The shotgun thundered, spitting death above me. The world went quiet as she closed in to finish me off.

When a familiar song cut through the night air. "*Gucci on a gator, Balmain on a bullfrog.*" A revving engine roared under it.

Stinko's sports car shot through the entrance, narrowly avoiding the fence. Dust rose in plumes from the whitewall tires. Daisy drove, both paws on the wheel, grinning as the wind stirred her fur. Stinko sat in the passenger seat, hooting as loud as he could. He spun to the side, pulling down his designer jeans as Daisy worked the wheel and put the car into a wild spin.

Stull looked at them, trying to swing her shotgun around in time. "What are they—"

Then Stinko unloaded his behind at her, Stanley, and Pomeroy. The most skunk ape stink that I've ever seen. Vast, gleaming ribbons of gunk that struck Stull center-mass, caught Pomeroy in the face, and hit Stanley as he managed to stand from his kick.

I was on them a moment later. Swinging my fist down, grabbing their guns—disarming them. The stench was unreal, but I didn't care. Dolly was at my side, whickering and snorting. She sunk her teeth into Stull's arm, stopping her from grabbing the shotgun, and I thanked her with a grunt as I hoisted the gun out of reach. She burbled, sickened by the stench too. Behind me, Daisy coasted the sports car to a halt. She and Stinko raced out, flashing their gleaming custom pieces, and covered the Aryan Race's finest until it was done.

Not that Stull and her boys were in much shape to do anything.

The skunk ape goop made them look they'd been caught in the eruption of a booger volcano. Pomeroy lay on his belly, retching. Stanley slumped back, blood from a busted nose adding some red to the green. Stull's entire face had been painted puke emerald—apart from her bright pink headband. The smell clawed at my nostrils too. I didn't vomit. Seeing the Volk Vanguard getting what was coming to them did wonders for my constitution.

Dolly snorted and did a little dance on her hooves, moving away from the stink. Had to be just as terrible for her. "Whoa." Stinko lowered his pistol. "Is that a—an alpaca?"

"Llama, babe," Daisy corrected. "How're you, Arlo?"

I grinned at them. "Never better."

The door creaked open. Dinah poked her head out. "Arlo?"

"It's okay." I waved to her. "They're friends! You and Caitlin should stay put until the cops get here. Hopefully, it won't be long." Stinko snorted at that—when the police showed up, he doubtlessly wanted to be elsewhere. But I wanted Stull and her friends hauled away in handcuffs and off the board.

The same with Mr. Grey.

"Gotta check on something." I slung the rifle over my back. The strap—made for a human's shoulder—dug in uncomfortably. "Keep Ms. Stull here covered." I walked back, patting Stinko. He looked back at me, his huge tail swishing back and forth like a merry dog.

I'd asked for help and he'd come through. For all my judgement, all my distaste about his country hip-hop music and Florida Man-style, Stinko had risked everything to save me.

While I got him deeper in trouble.

I stopped by the gate. Mr. Grey's Range Rover was gone, Mr. Grey and his sword with it. All that was left was a puddle of blood on the ground—and a lumpy, fuzzy gray sausage lying in the dirt. A severed finger.

One of Candlewick Ranch's goats trotted over, gave the finger a sniff, and started munching. A few bites and it vanished in the goat's quivering muzzle.

"Holy Woods," I muttered—and then a pair of headlights flashed over me. I shielded my eyes from the light as the car pulled in.

Ollie Candle was behind the wheel.

I returned his rifle to him and walked him back to the ranch house. Daisy and Stinko stood guard over Stull and her goons, who were too busy gagging to offer much protest. Ollie watched as the door opened and then saw Dinah and Caitlin standing there, framed in the porchlights. He ran to them, dashing past the chaos of his yard, and wrapped his arms around his family. Candle was shaking. Fear, relief, love—all making him quiver. Human love couldn't be denied.

I padded over to join them.

Candle looked back at me and wiped his eyes on his sleeve. "They're all right. They're safe." He stared at Stull and the others and at me. "Why?"

"Because they heard you were waffling. Rusk, Special Agent Rod Todd. This real estate man named Walter Rose, over in Terroir Valley." I brought him up to speed. The truth behind Prop 33 and the Northern California Development Corridor that would wipe away his ranch and the wolves in one blow. He stared in silent horror, his arm still around Caitlin. When I finished, Bandit was licking his fingers. "You got any proof?"

The recording that Rose had swiped.

"Proof?" Dinah waved to the Volk Vanguard. "There's your proof. Arlo saved us, Ollie. Doesn't that earn him some trust?"

Candle sighed. "Yeah. Of course. This thing with the wolves—it got me all mixed up. Keeping this place running was hard enough. When I imagined predators going after the goats, putting my family in danger—and maybe this whole area getting swept away—I didn't know what to do. And Jerome was there, urging me not to back down." Regret clung to each word. "But he didn't have to do much to convince me."

"I know, man," I agreed. "Same with me and Rose."

"My dad used to work with sheep. He'd have a goat join the herd—the Judas Goat. The sheep would trust him. Come slaughtering time, the Judas Goat would lead them right down the chute to their death." He looked at Dinah. "That's what I've been. The Rangers—they might end up going to prison. Or worse. All because I wanted to do something crazy."

"But you can stop it," Caitlin said. "Right? You can get them to go home?"

"Once I tell them the truth about Prop 33, about Jerome, you better believe it." He offered a sad smile. "We'll figure something else out. Another way to deal with the wolves."

"That llama seems to be doing a pretty good job." I pointed to Dolly, who was sputtering, trying to get rid of Stinko's spray. "Deserves a forest-burning medal."

My phone buzzed. Unknown number. I left the Candles to their happy reunion as I stepped back onto the leaf-strewn driveway. "Arlo Patches." It was Lloyd Rusk. The ringmaster of the whole circus. His voice drifted in across the phone line, self-satisfied and oozing politico charm. "How's your Halloween going?"

"Spooky," I said. "How's yours?"

"I'm enjoying it well enough—from Walter Rose's vineyard." Where my family was. "I heard you were just here?"

"That's right. But I didn't like it, so I left. Too scary for me."

"Is that so?" We were sparring—dancing around the threats and violence that were soon to follow. Young bucks clicking antlers, without making the full charge—not yet. "Well, I apologize. I think one of my associates might have frightened you a little."

"Or didn't scare me enough."

"Maybe I can change your mind, then? You swing back here, forget this case, and I'll double whatever fee that Rose was gonna fork over. I don't deal in fun-sized candy bars. My friends get the big ones. How's that sound?"

He'd tried to have me killed. Now he was trying to bribe me.

It wouldn't work.

"No thanks. I'm trying to cut down on my sugar." I grunted. "I'm watching my weight."

"It's a fortune, Arlo. And all you gotta do is walk away." His voice tightened. Some of his confidence slipping as the fancy chitchat vanished. "Don't deal with the Rangers. Don't worry about the wolves. Just stick to your family, go home, and stay hidden. Isn't what your people are good at?"

I glanced at Ollie Candle, still with his arm around Dinah. "I think it's a little late for that. Candle knows you were playing him. I don't think he appreciates it. The Volk Vanguard are soon to be in custody, and they're gonna make a nice little Nazi choir in my brother's jail. They'll give up Wambach, and I bet he'll give up you." I hooted. "Your little conspiracy's falling to pieces."

Silence on the line. I didn't like that sound. Stinko looked up from guarding the Volk Vanguard.

Maybe I was the one who had overplayed his hand.

"You know who else is with me, enjoying Halloween at Rose Petal Winery?"

I did. Rosemary, Freshta, Harriet—and Milo.

"You harm a hair of their fur and I'll—"

"Come down to the vineyard, Arlo, and we'll talk about it." Rusk laughed dryly. As much humor in his voice as a shotgun. "I'll tell you a horror story. The Bigfoot Who Knew Too Much. Just wait until I get to the ending. You'll learn what happened to his family. It'll keep you up at night, I promise you that."

I roared, blood-pounding, teeth-flashing. It took everything I had not to send the cell phone shattering against a nearby tree trunk. I hung up instead.

Stinko looked at me, tail arched. "What's up, man?"

"Rusk's trying to lure me back. My family's there."

"He'll be waiting," Daisy said. "A trap."

"I know. I don't care." I pocketed the phone and looked over the weapons that the Volk Vanguard had brought to play. Selected a revolver and shoved that into my jeans. "I'm going back."

Candle had been listening. "You want help?"

Simple as that. "Appreciate it, but you need to get back to the State Park and send your friends home before Halloween ends. Make sure they don't do anything stupid to Jerome, either." Something told me the Rangers wouldn't be happy when they discovered their friend had set them up. "Take Dinah and the kid with you, just in case." But even that might not be enough. "Daisy and Stinko—you ought to go too." It was the next best thing after Dolly the llama.

"No." Stinko walked toward me, grinning—showing off the gold on his teeth. "You and me, Arlo. We're together on this." He offered his fist. "No such thing as Alpha Wolves. I get it. But packs are real. I'm running in yours."

I looked at Daisy—as if asking for permission. She shrugged—Stinko was old enough to make his own decision. "You two have fun. Don't stay out too late."

Stinko might dress in designer finery and make groan-inducing music, but he could scrap. And another reason I needed him—my wheels were back at the winery. Stinko's sports car offered a fast way back to Terroir Valley.

And I had always liked Stinko.

I bumped his fist back. "We ought to pick up some costumes on the way—hard as that may be, with them already sold out. See if we can blend in with the crowd."

"Way ahead of you." Stinko paused to give Daisy a nuzzle and darted back to his car. Sirens wailed in the distance—my brother's deputies, coming to pick up the Neo-Nazis. Stinko popped the trunk and I joined him. A pair of oversized masks.

Werewolf masks.

"Perfect." I snagged the masks and we set off.

The two of us rolled silently through the streets of Terroir Valley. All around us, Halloween revelry packed both sides of the street. The school age Trick-Or-Treaters had given way to costumed adults, who put the kids to shame with their antics. Slap a mask on a human and they'll jump at the chance to act like an animal.

But at least they were after the joys of alcohol, costume contests, and EDM-powered October raves rather than bigfoot blood—unlike Lloyd Rusk and his goons. Stinko screeched to a halt at an intersection as a costumed pub crawl burst out of a high-end wine bar on its way to the next watering hole. A bunch of humans in banana, zombie, and t-rex costumes spotted us and start howling in joy. Stinko and I looked at them.

That's when they realized that we had fur all over our bodies—not just the werewolf masks on our heads.

They shut up quick and we rolled on.

"You got a plan, Arlo?" Stinko hadn't put on his music. Didn't even touch the radio. I was grateful for that. "We getting your family out of there or are we out for blood?"

"My family's safety comes first." I snapped out the phone. So far, I'd sent three texts to Harold, but hadn't heard back. The guy was involved in a standoff with the Jefferson Rangers—who were hopefully surrendering. He probably wasn't checking his phone. By the time he did, and brought the county cops down to Terroir Valley, it might already be too late. "We get them out of there. Then we go for blood."

Stinko had his fancy pistol resting on his lap. "Hell yeah."

"Turn here. Park in the first place you can."

We went up the slope leading to the Rose Petal Winery. Past the long tangle of vineyards and the glowing Jack-O-Lanterns leering at us from the fence posts. A packed parking lot waited by the House of Blood Red Roses, which gleamed in ghostly green and shocking crimson lights. A big crowd, many in costumes, gathered outside for their chance to enter the spooky maze and get the crap scared out of them.

I was running against a different kind of terror.

Stinko and I got out and joined the crowd. I scanned the mass of mummies, mutants, ghosts, cheerleaders, pirates, and even some tasteless dude dressed as a bigfoot—or maybe a gorilla—for any sign of Rosemary and the others.

No luck.

My heart pounded worse. Fear trickling cold as Halloween carnival music lilted. Scarecrows watched from the edges of the House of Blood Red Roses, smiles stitched on burlap faces like they were enjoying the show. Stinko and I forced our way through the crowd, getting a few costume compliments and some annoyed insults as we cut in line. The world seemed to swirl and dance, flickering in through the eyeholes of my mask as the beating I'd taken earlier took its toll.

No Rosemary, Harriet, Freshta, or Milo. Like I was trapped in a nightmare.

"Mr. Patches!" A scared voice. I spun around. One small vampire cowgirl stood at the edge of the crowd, standing tall in her boots. Maris. I hurried over and Stinko followed. She must have recognized me, even with the werewolf mask. Well, how many squatches were there in Terroir Valley? "Mr. Patches—

Arlo—" She reached me.

"Maris. What's going on?" Would she know where my family was? "Where's your dad?"

"He's—he's in the house." She nodded toward the mansion. "I was grounded, but snuck out. He'll probably ground me for like a month after this—but I don't give a damn." I approved. "He was talking to his friend, Mr. Rusk—he seemed really upset. My dad did too." She jammed her hands in her pocket. A nervous vampire cowgirl. "I—I don't know what to do, Arlo."

"Stay close," I said, as a sharp tang of cologne joined the candy apples and popcorn.

Rusk.

He came walking through the crowd, wearing the same simple business suit. His only concession to the season was an evil clown mask, all snarling teeth and pale skin, which he ripped off as he approached. Mr. Grey loomed next to him, still in his highland fling outfit. He had thick bandages around his arm and made a fist as he and Rusk joined me.

I moved in front of Maris. "Where are they?" I asked.

"Who?" Rusk asked. "Oh—your band." A sly smile. "I think they went into the haunted house. Rose sent them a little early. A special Halloween treat." He flashed his palms—his voice going dry with sarcasm. "Hope nothing in there's too scary."

My nostrils flared, the wolf mask pressing my warm breath to my face. "If anything happens to them—"

"What are you gonna do? Pound your chest, Mr. King Kong?" It takes a certain kind of Harrower to stay brave in the face of an angry bigfoot, but I had the feeling Rusk was incapable of feeling fear. "Go ahead. Raise Hell. Prop 33's already on the ballot. Our little show at the state forest served its purpose. The Rangers can even go home now. Media's juicing the story. My government cronies will spin it right and I'll flood the airwaves and mailboxes of this state with ads. Prop 33 is pro-environment. Prop 33 is pro-worker. Prop 33 supports small business. Prop 33 is all-American. Prop 33 is—you get the idea." He slid the mask over his face again, transforming into the creepy clown. "Selling a story. It's how humanity works. Welcome to the jungle, Mr. Patches. You never stood a chance."

I grabbed him by the throat. Gasps and delighted screams from the costumed crowd. They must think this was all part of the show. Rusk gagged and flailed his arms and legs—a puppet in a psycho's hands. Then I roared loud enough to drown out the piped-in spooky music and sent Rusk flying.

He soared over the crowd and smashed into the collection of scarecrows. Maris screamed. Stinko let out a frightened mew and Mr. Grey just stared at me. None of them quite believed what had happened.

I lowered my hand, fingers shaking. Rusk had landed in the scarecrows. I'd broken a few—bowling for Halloween decorations. It was the wrong move. I'd turned into the squatch that these people feared.

A forest monster.

Something else I'd done—I'd broken cover. Assaulting Rusk had crossed a line. Now Mr. Grey had all the right in the world to strike back.

He did, overcoming his surprise and drawing the claymore, just as Stinko seemed to realize that the spell had broken and pulled his golden pistol from inside the satin of his designer jacket. He had it halfway out, gilded gator barrel extended just as Mr. Grey's sword rushed up in a lethal slash.

Caught the pistol's barrel, wedged it up, wrenching it from Stinko's hands. It went soaring into the air. A silver shooting star.

Then Mr. Grey spun the sword around, going for a slash on Stinko himself. "Pull a gun on me! Big man's asking for it—"

"Stinko!" I grabbed him by the tail and pulled. Stinko squealed and went with me, the sword humming down and slicing into his wolf mask—just missing his face. The rubber fell away, revealing his terrified, tattooed face. Then we were running, shoving our way through the crowd, and dashing for the gothic entrance of the haunted house. Maris screamed too and slipped between a pirate and a Grim Reaper, losing herself in the crowd. Probably a smart move.

Running into the haunted house—with Mr. Grey charging behind us—certainly wasn't.

But my family was in there and I needed to find them.

We dashed into the entrance. I lunged back, grabbed the door with one hand and pulled my pistol with the other. Slammed the door shut. Stinko found a leering gargoyle on a pedestal of stone-colored Styrofoam and sent it crashing down to block the door. Temporary obstacle. Then both of us loped ahead as pounding and hacking noises came from the door.

We dashed down a long hall. Ghostly green wine bottles floated across the wall, hidden projectors making them dance. A nasty sulfur scent cut the air. Not from the house.

"You okay?"

"Just dropped some in my pants." Stinko sighed. "Involuntary defense mechanism."

"Can you make more? Maybe give Mr. Grey a blast?"

"I'm fresh out, bro. Sorry."

I looked at the pistol. A revolver, in bad condition. I snapped open the cylinder. One shot inside. That was it.

Shooting it at Mr. Grey would probably just make him mad.

Behind us, wood cracked. Hinges screeched. Mr. Grey had entered.

The two of us turned and ran, dashing down the darkened hallway, trying to find my family. A stairwell in front of us—and then a booming laugh and a dark shape with a silvery glisten slid into our path. I hoisted up the revolver on instinct and fired—blasting a hole through a robot vampire rigged from the wall, wielding a pair of fake garden shears.

The gunshot echoed through the hall, putting an ache in my ears, followed by a tinny mechanized laugh, repeated endlessly. "I need your blood to make my wine-wine-wine-wine—"

"Shut up!" Stinko smashed the vamp pruner down and we kept going.

No bullets left.

Ran to the second level—a gothic hall of mirrors. Three large shapes in the low light, reflecting a thousand times in distorted, mixed-up ways. Sunshine cut through a dense canopy and burned bright in my heart as I hurried over. Rosemary, Harriet, and Freshta. But then the fear came back, strong as ever, as I realized something else.

No Milo.

Rosemary spun around. "Arlo—" The joy leaving her as she saw my fear. "What's wrong?"

"We're in danger. All of us." Soon as I said that, Freshta pulled her machete. "No time to explain. That Scottish squatch is—" I stopped. Where was Mr. Grey? He'd cut through the doorway. Was he coming up the stairs? Stinko had gone there, squaring his shoulders—but no Mr. Grey. "Where's Milo?"

Harriet hastened to the door at the end of the hall. A winding stairwell, leaving the House of Blood Red Roses and cutting down to the graveyard by the stables—the outdoor portion of the spookhouse. "He went ahead, promising to trigger the scares." She hesitated. "I think he's braver than all of us."

He'd gone ahead—into the Woods only knew what sort of danger.

Then the wall next to us broke to pieces. The flimsy funhouse mirror shattered into a blizzard of glass. Most of them went slicing into me. A dozen little stings. Glass jabbing into my arms, my belly, cutting a groove across my forehead. They sparkled and shone as they stabbed home, and I got to see my face reflected at me a dozen times, all lit up in a sickly ghoulish green glow.

Countless pinpricks of pain. A million bee stings.

Mr. Grey followed through the shattered mirror, claymore raised. He must've scaled the wall and smashed his way in. Now his sword came down. Aiming straight at my skull.

Freshta's machete caught it, turned it, and sent it crashing down.

Metal rang on metal. Mr. Grey's sword was bigger, bulkier, and stronger—

but Freshta still held him back as I wrenched a metal shard as big as a squirrel tail from my forearm and charged. "Stinko!" I cried out as blood welled up in my fur, crimsoning an eye. "Get Rosemary and Harriet out of here!" I rammed the spiky section down, driving it into Mr. Grey's shoulder as deep as it would go. It cut my fingers. I didn't care.

He wailed. Pulled the sword back and Freshta advanced.

Harriet screeched. Rosemary called out—but Stinko was grabbing their arms, dragging them down the stairs. Getting them to safety.

Freshta and I fought together. My fists and her machete. A wild fight. A sasquatch fight. I drove a powerful fist into Mr. Grey's belly and caught the basket hilt of his claymore against my jaw. She parried his next blow and used the length of her machete to draw a red line across his fancy outfit. He grunted and roared and kept fighting.

We battled like wounded animals when there's no sense, no thinking—nothing but the need to fight and win and survive.

The claymore jabbed out. Slashed my arm deep—but went too far. Smashed through another mirror and wedged into the wall. Mr. Grey roared and pulled it back—only for Freshta to take some meat from his arm with her machete. He pulled the arm back, leaving the sword, and tackled her.

They crashed to the ground together. Mr. Grey had his knees on her belly, his fists up—raining down blows. The machete rattled away.

He wasn't going to choke the life out of her. He was going to beat her to death.

I stumbled closer, clutching my bleeding arm—trying to help. Stumbled instead. Bumped into a bedsheet ghost with a face frozen in a wail, set over a glowing orb. I looked at the ghost. It was screaming at me.

I pulled it free, ripping it away from the prop. Bundled it over my arm. Ran to Mr. Grey and pulled the sheet over his head.

He was blinded. Gagged. He snorted and roared. Rolled over, trying to pull the bedsheet free. I held it fast.

Freshta hit him under the sheet—again and again. He was off her, springing up, trying to shake me off. I was wrestling an earthquake. Muffled roars and snarls from under the sheet as he bucked—but I had my arms around him, pulling the sheet down. Freshta kept the punches going, and then he was moving, running to the side—trying to pull free.

I didn't just let it happen. I helped. Freshta did too.

We rammed him straight into the far wall.

His skull smashed through plywood and plaster. Thudded into something solid. He grunted again and tried to free himself—but Mr. Grey was stuck.

Freshta snarled. Grabbed the machete.

"No." I spat the word out through bloodied teeth. "No one dies tonight."

She hissed at me in some foreign language and grabbed a length of solid pipe from a gothic organ worked into the far wall. "I'll—I'll get Milo," I said, as she wrenched it free. "Get to the others. Then we go. Okay?"

"Okay." She nodded to me and brought the metal pipe onto Mr. Grey's arms—one and then the other. Breaking them to be sure. A sound like clear wood snapping under water. "Harriet—she has a good brother." That was probably the best compliment I'd get from Freshta—and I was happy to get it.

"She's got a good girlfriend too." I wiped the blood from my eyes and dashed down the hall as she moved to Mr. Grey's legs.

Halloween wasn't over yet.

Outside, in the graveyard, my worst fears came to life. No Milo. No sign of anything, in the haze of artificial fog. "Milo!" I managed to shout his name as I vaulted over a length of graves. Hint of his smell—well-seasoned with sugar and chocolate from a night of Halloween sweets—but no cub. I stumbled around fake stone angels, dragging myself along. After getting beaten into unconsciousness by Mr. Grey, the gunfight at Candlewick Ranch, and the showdown in the haunted house, I had nothing left.

Nothing that could have stopped the boot ramming into my spine and planting me on the dusty ground.

"Arlo Patches!" Wambach towered above me. He wore a skull mask, but there was no disguising his bulk. Or his menace.

I twisted around, forced away the pounding in my skull to look at him. He carried a long-barreled pistol in one hand. A huge combat knife in the other. He had the gun aimed at my head.

"Was hoping I'd run into you." He needn't have bothered with the gun. At the moment, I couldn't lift a pinecone.

"Wambach…"

"You looking for Milo?" Dark shapes behind him, cutting through the mist like phantoms. The Storm Battalion. His Oregon Nazi commando back-up. "Don't worry. He's next. But I want you." He forced his boot in my spine. "We're already in a graveyard, ain't we?"

"Don't—don't hurt him—"

"Brother." He leaned down. "I'll do whatever I want. You see, Bigfoot or humans, we're all animals. Animal kingdom's about hierarchy. And when you're the Alpha? You get to call the shots."

AND ALL OF ROSE'S HORSES CAME CHARGING OUT OF THE STABLES...

Milo's smell deepened. I looked up. Glanced at a gravestone, artistically leaning to the side against another—giving the fake graveyard a purposeful look of neglect.

Milo was under it. Watching me with eyes as big as the moon.

I forced my gaze away. Forced myself to be quiet.

"All right, Arlo. We've talked enough. Get ready to go to bigfoot heaven."

Come on, furball. Run. Run away and don't look back.

But he didn't run.

Instead, Milo Sang.

The words came out, clear and strong. Cutting through the piped-in Halloween music like a giant bell had been struck. Wambach winced—the frequency painfully high. The Storm Battalion soldiers bristled.

Something in the stables broke. Whickering cut across the graveyard.

And all of Rose's horses came charging across, cutting through the mock tombstones in a torrent of pounding hooves and shaking manes.

It was all I needed. I reared up. Forced away his boot with strength I didn't know I had left and managed a flailing, wild punch. A glancing blow to his face—but a glancing blow from a squatch is no joke. He went sprawling. Then I was running to Milo, helping him up, shielding him from the Storm Battalion as hooves churned the earth. "Run!" I shouted to him, shoving him past the tombstones as a charging mare galloped past. He did so, his cloak billowing, his Sherlock Holmes hat falling away.

I spun around. No Wambach—but Tugg of the Storm Battalion was there, leveling his rifle.

A bullet cut him down first, blasting into his shoulder and dropping him.

Galloping horses, dust, mist—and more gunfire. Clear, precise shots coming from the hillside.

Freshta, saving my furry behind once again.

I ran. Hurried up the stairs after Milo while gunshots burned behind me and horses whinnied. Freshta had perched on the top of the hill, lying on her belly with her scoped rifle. She fired again as I ran past, cutting down the Storm Battalion one by one. Maybe going for non-lethal shots. Maybe not. I didn't particularly care.

I passed her. Made it to the top.

Then Rosemary was next to me, helping me stand. A new sort of light had joined the Halloween display—berry flash of cop cars. They formed a ring, the customers for the House of Blood Red Roses scrambling away. Harold and some of his deputies were making their way through them, fighting the crowd—heading toward the two small figures standing in front of the house.

Maris and Milo? She was holding his hand. Protecting him.

Humans—they can certainly surprise you.

THERE'S NO SUCH THING AS ALPHAS

Monday of the following week. November 5. Election Day. I'd been tasked with taking Milo to school—just to check in with his teacher and pick up the week's homework. His parents were keeping him home and I didn't blame them. Busy as beavers at dam building time too. Harold was knee-deep in police work and Rosemary was besieged by reporters. Slipping Milo out to give him a break—and a chance to see his friends at school—was one good thing I could do for them.

I walked him in, picked up the schoolwork, let him trade tales of Halloween chaos with his buddies, and then shepherded him out back to the car during pick-up time. I wasn't alone. The last bell had rung and clusters of parents and kids headed out for their own cars and the commute home under a gray November sky.

Milo paused as he gripped the door of my pick-up. His arm waved crazily. "Caitlin!"

She was across from him, getting into her dad's SUV. And there he was, Ollie Candle, wearing a simple camo hunter's jacket. Caitlin dashed over before he could stop her.

Their stories flew like falling leaves in autumn. "I was attacked in a haunted house—and then I ran into a graveyard, and summoned a herd of horses, and then my aunt's girlfriend was firing with a sniper rifle and—"

"My mom had a rifle too, and fought off these guys who were at my house, and then our llama attacked them, and a skunk ape showed up in a sports car—"

Both were as excited as only kids can be when they got a good story.

Ollie and I looked on fondly and then we stared at each other. "How're things?" I asked.

He shrugged. "Trial's coming up. The reveal that Jerome was a snitch—and that he was the loudest voice for the occupation—is muddling up the prosecution considerably. The fact that nobody died helps too." He paused, scratching stubble. "I've got you to thank for that."

"You don't have to thank me for anything." I'd caused the whole mess in the first place—and I hadn't ended it. "Have you voted?"

"Planning to swing by the polling station at the high school right now. No on Prop 33."

"That's the spirit."

But would it matter? Lloyd Rusk had been working hard, blanketing the states in positive messaging about the Northern California Development Corridor. He promised jobs, cheap housing, green energy, and everything and a slice of cake if you bubbled in Yes on Proposition 33. Harriet had managed to do a few interviews, but his talking heads were lined up to counter every argument.

And as for Walter Rose—the one person whose testimony could throw a wrench in Rusk's plans? He was gone. His daughter too. Both just vanished. Maybe they were on a plane to some offshore tax haven in the Caribbean. Maybe they were hiding out in San Francisco. In any case, he wasn't talking.

Candle looked back at the kids. "I don't know if we're ever gonna solve anything. Me and you—I don't know. But their generation? The best we can do is give them a chance."

He offered his hand, and I shook it.

Then Milo piled into the car, and I sped away, hitting the freeway for the ride back to Harold's house.

We cruised through light traffic. I'd substituted news updates for my usual Outlaw Country on the radio. The election results trickling in did nothing to soothe my nerves. Plenty of other measures on the ballot, plenty of new candidates looking to mark their territory on some office or another, and Prop 33 was just another ingredient in the mix. Milo settled silently into the passenger and looked like he wanted to say something but thought better of it.

Then my phone buzzed.

I'd kept it on, just in case Harold or Rosemary or Harriet needed me, but the caller ID was for someone else: Dr. Braithwaite. I snapped it on.

"Yeah?"

"Patches—thank God. I know where the Roses are." Holy Woods. My fingers tightened on the steering wheel. "Maris just called me. She snuck her dad's phone and got the message out. Sent me their coordinates." Dr. Braithwaite's words came in a breathless rush. "She thinks they're in danger."

"Where?"

"The State Forest. I'll text you the coordinates." Then, a moment of hesitation. "Arlo—if I tell you where they are, will you help them?"

Would I help them? Walter Rose had lied to me. He'd used me for his own purposes that put a torch to the entire forest—and when I found out, he tried to have me killed by that psycho squatch Scotsman. Now, the other thieves in his gang were getting angry, turning on them, putting his family into the fire—and it was up to me to pull them from the blaze.

I looked at Milo. He had overheard the whole conversation, and I knew what he would say even before the words left his mouth.

“Uncle Arlo…” He shifted in his seat, a scrap of fur in a blue polo shirt, blue hoodie jacket, and cargo shorts, who still had the innocence of things that are young and wild. “She helped me. Maris Rose protected me.”

The coordinates appeared on my phone. Not so far away. The Roses hadn’t stayed close. The exit waited up ahead. I looked at the clear, cold fall sky just beginning to deepen with early darkness, and the golden leaves dancing in the wind stirred by passing cars. What had Ollie Candle said?

That the best we could do was give the next generation a chance.

I took the next exit.

I needed to make a decision as I parked at the entrance of an ancient logging road running through the Charles E. Boles State Forest. Would Milo come with me or stay in the car, alone, on a dark road, with dangers to his family still lurking? Of course, there was no telling what was waiting for us when we found the Roses. Still, I’d rather he was close by. Besides, we were in the woods.

It was my natural habitat.

“Where are they?” Milo darted along at my side. “Are we gonna see any animals? Maybe I could, you know, talk to them?”

I put a finger to my lips. “Come on, furball. You’re a bigfoot. Time to be quiet.”

That’s when we heard it. A powerful noise, lilting and yet drifting over everything. The wind learning to speak.

Wolf howls.

Milo gasped. A shiver had to be trickling down his spine, same as mine. But he knew enough to be quiet. Maybe they were close by. Maybe something had agitated them. The sound seemed to come from everywhere at once and I couldn’t pick out wolf in the wild bouquet of scents.

So we went further on, into the country of wolves. Off the trail and to the banks of a creek flowing fast thanks to autumnal downpours. I knew this stream, from the slick stones poking up from the water to the leaves zooming along the surface like colorful boats. I’d drank this water, splashed in it, swam when I was bold enough to dare the cold. Now, I stepped carefully along its banks until we neared a clearing at the foot of a jagged promontory of gray stone. That section of mountain looked over everything—a wise, ancient protector.

Right now, it looked down at a fancy campsite. Domed REI tent and matching stove by the fire. Walter Rose was at the blaze, fiddling with something and mumbling. Maris sat on a rock, looking as miserable as only a thirteen-year-old girl could manage. Both wore puffy North Face jackets.

"Maris!" Milo called to her, ruining our approach.

She perked up. "Mr. Patches—Milo!"

But Walter noticed us too. He forgot about the fire and dove for the shelter of the tent, where a duffel bag waited. His hand reached inside, pulling out a thick automatic pistol. He tumbled toward us, stumbling in his hiking boots, and trying to swing up the pistol.

Reminded me of a frightened roly-poly.

But a fool with a pistol is still dangerous.

"Walter—Walter—easy!" I showed my hands and Milo did the same. "We're here to help you."

"Is that so?" Rose made it to his feet, pistol extended in one hand. "So what is this, huh? This ambush?" He gestured with the pistol, and I carefully stepped in front of Milo. "How'd you find out where we were hiding anyway?"

"Dad." Maris's face split into a sad scowl—a mix of embarrassment and fright. "Dad—I called them." He stared at her. "Or I called Dr. Braithwaite. And she called them."

He looked at her in disbelief. "Why?"

"Because you need help, dad." Maris waved her hands at the trees. "What are we supposed to do? Live in the forest forever? We're not sasquatches. And you know you can't trust that Rusk guy. He's sent his goon after us. We need to stop running—and you need to tell the truth." Another sigh. "That gun is isn't even loaded."

He looked at the pistol, a confused squint showing that she was right. "What—"

Another howl hit the air. Closer this time.

"Something must be scaring them," Milo said.

I crossed the campsite. Walter still aimed his pistol at me, and when that didn't stop me, he stumbled his way back until he was lost in the shade of the trees. Red and gold leaves crunched under his boots. "Walter." I tried to make myself look less scary. A nice, friendly bigfoot. "Your daughter's got more sense than you. Time to hang it up. You do what's right, maybe you'll get to keep the winery. Maybe you'll stay out of jail—and more than that, you'll be safe."

"What the hell do you know about it?"

"I know about second chances, Walter." I put my hands in the pockets of my windbreaker. "That's for certain."

He lowered the useless gun and slumped on a broken log.

That's what saved him from a burst of automatic gunfire, which cut through the air where his head had just been. The shots shredded a tree trunk and sent leaves tumbling down. Rose dropped with a gasp and my legs tensed, getting ready to run.

Wambach walked out from the trees.

He wore woodland cameo and a watch cap, like some soldier from an unknown army, a sleek assault rifle coming up to cover us. No need to shoot at us from cover now. He could close in and do his killing up close. He pushed Rose aside, aiming the rifle up at me. "Stop!" I froze up. Couldn't reach the kids. Then he shifted his gun and aimed at Maris.

And Milo.

"You make any noise at all, you try any of that sasquatch magic mumbo-jumbo, I will sink a hollow point round right into your furry face. You got me?"

The cub stayed silent.

Then Wambach pointed the rifle back at me. "I'm wiping out all of you. Right now. Rose was the target. You're just a bonus."

"Please..." Rose begged. He must know that it wouldn't do any good, but it was all he had left. "My daughter—"

"A witness. She'll go too." Wambach spat on the dried leaves below him as something rustled in the wood nearby. "You shouldn't be surprised. I'm the best hunter in the animal kingdom. The Alpha. And that's why I'm going to wipe you out."

Another wolf howl.

"What is—are you doing that?" He shouted at Milo.

The kid, terrified, shook his head.

"Then what—"

Maris pointed.

A trio of wolf cubs had emerged from the trees and started pawing along the edge of the camp. Walter Rose's campfire cooking must have attracted them. They were fuzzy and small, as adorable as only puppies could be, with marble gray fuzz and huge dark eyes. Little yips mixed with the rush of the stream as they bounded closer, driven by pure curiosity about the exciting new smells.

Wambach stared. "What the hell?" He stomped his foot on the ground, making the wolf cubs whimper. "Go on! Get out of there!"

A growl came from the darkness.

"You don't get it." I tensed up. Readied weary muscles for one last go. "We are in the animal kingdom. You don't threaten a creature's young without consequence." The mommy and daddy wolves emerged from under the trees. "And there's no such things as Alphas."

The wolf got the back of his leg, just behind the knee. Up close, you got to see how big they were, and how fast, and how powerful. Teeth bit deep into Wambach's leg, ripping through his jeans and his flesh and probably scraping bone. Blood came down in rivers. Wambach dropped to a kneel, wolf teeth fixed deep. Another wolf, a silvery ghost, crept in from the side, dashing protectively in front of the cubs and giving us a big growl.

But Wambach still had the gun.

I crossed the campsite, heart pounding. Even with a wolf snacking on him, he managed to grit his teeth and push the rifle toward me. I lunged out. My fingers slipped on the barrel as he tried to force it down, his finger curling on the trigger. A bullet hummed out. Semi-auto. Close enough to make all hearing vanish from my ears and paint the world in white. Somewhere, far away, Milo and Maris were screaming.

I tightened my grip. I pulled. Wambach roared at me, and I roared back.

Then I had the gun free, wrenched out of his hands and leaving a finger twisted. He jabbed his elbow down, caught the back of the wolf and making it finally let go, then reached for his belt where a nasty hunting knife waited.

Shoot him? Instinct told me to do something else.

I hoisted up the rifle and smashed the butt into his face. He managed to hoist up a hand, sort of deflect the blow, but something still cracked. So I swung the rifle around, used it like a clumsy baseball bat in another thwack to the side of his skull. He had the knife out now, the blade shining in fall sunlight. Holy Woods—how much punishment could this guy take?

He was tough as the mountains. That was for sure.

Managed to stand up now, pulling the knife back for a stab. I hoisted the rifle over my head, tensed my muscles, and brought it down dead center into his face just as he lashed out with the knife. Something in the rifle broke. Mechanical bits jangled down.

His stab sliced air. The knife dropped.

Then he did too.

That left the wolf. Its teeth bared, its ears tented, legs angled for a deadly jump. Another appeared behind it, black-furred—a storm cloud that had fallen to earth and now stalked the woods. I looked back at the father wolf, taking him in for the first time. A big, old grayback, with a constellation of scars across his muzzle and a half-chewed ear, looked at me with eyes like gold stars. A deep canine musk, woodsy and thick, came from the wolf in waves, mixed with iron from the blood in his teeth.

How long had this old hunter walked the woods? Did he know that he was traveling in a new place now, where his ancestors had once been hunted to extinction?

If he did, he probably didn't care. The threat to his family was all that mattered.

And after Wambach, my friends and I were the ones causing trouble.

I hoisted up my hands. Grunted. Tried to make myself as non-threatening as possible.

But the growls still came from the lead wolf and his black-furred brother or sister. Both, pawing closer. Wambach lay between us, blood still seeping from his leg. Had I killed him with that swing? His chest still rose and fell—I'd just busted him up good. Too bad. Would the wolves munch on him after they attacked us? That might be some consolation.

I looked back at the camp. Maris, Milo, and Walter all stayed together—Maris again defending my nephew while Walter had gone in front of both. The humans' eyes had grown wide, their faces drained of color. Milo's fur stood up and he shook. The fear of being hunted, of encountering something in the woods that could give you a run for your money—every species had that.

But beyond that fear, in the eyes of the children, there was something else.

Wonder.

Milo slid away from Maris. "Milo—what are you—" She reached for his arm, but he scrambled away from her and hopped onto a stump near their camp stove.

"Furball." I hooted low. "Get out of here."

He shook his head. "This is what I have to do."

Then he threw back his head and Sang.

It wasn't the wild, frightened, and instinctual song that he'd made in the chaos of battle on Halloween night, or the snap decision cry that he'd pulled off to make the Candle's llama stop wailing on me. Instead, this was a song that came deep from his heart, a clear, echoing strand of wild birdsong that looped and twisted like the wind through the trees or a stream through the mountains. It was everything wild. The clatter of deer hooves and the chatter of possums.

The howling of wolves.

The wolf ears tented. The papa wolf and his younger brother or son listened carefully. The mother and the cubs did too. The smaller of the cubs even yipped back. Perhaps trying to converse with Milo's song.

Milo kept going, pausing for breath, and continuing to Sing. He had his arms awkwardly at his sides, his head held high, singing his heart out.

Then, his song drifted off and ended.

The wolves looked at him for a few more seconds. The old father turned away and snorted. He made a sort of half-whine, half-bark, and his storm cloud buddy followed him down the trail. The mother and the cubs joined them, all loping away. Her pale pelt, shimmering and bright, danced amongst the darkened boughs and fall leaves like some spirit, something magical, leaving the world of living things and dancing into the Holy Groves beyond.

Then they were gone.

For a while, we were silent. We had seen something magical. No—two things. Maris stared at Milo. "How—how did you do that?"

"I'm a Singer," he explained. "It's a special bigfoot thing. A power we once had." He hopped down from the stump and went to stand next to me. "I guess it came back."

"I guess so," I said. Wambach groaned. I kicked his face and sent his spittle into the grass. "Maris, does your boot have shoelaces?"

"Yeah?"

"Go ahead and pull them out. I'm gonna tie this guy up." Then I faced Walter. He looked like he wanted to turn into a worm and burrow under the earth. "You need to call the police."

"But—"

"It's your only chance." I showed some teeth. Maybe I could be a bit of a wolf too. "Your daughter's only chance. Rusk won't stop until you're shut up for good. You'll only be safe if he's in jail and that means revealing everything. Try to get him and his bosses on the hook." It was a long shot, of course. "You know it and I know it. So call up the police and tell them you've got a true blue Nazi outlaw trussed up and ready for capture and you're willing to turn yourself in and cooperate."

He looked at his hiking shoes.

Maris handed me her bootlaces. Bright pink. "Dad." She spoke earnestly, without a trace of adolescent snark. "He saved us."

Walter Rose sighed. Then reached for his phone and dialed 911.

I hogtied Wambach. I even found Rose's first aid kit and did my best to staunch the bleeding on his leg. An Old West term came to mind: cheating the hangman. I wouldn't let Wambach do that. How long until his consciousness trickled back? Hopefully, by the time it did, we'd all be far away, and he'd be bound for a secure jail cell. Then he could go back to prison for good. He'd done enough damage.

When it was done, I walked back to Milo, who was sitting with Maris on the tree stump. They'd managed to get the fire going again, and each had some marshmallows on skewers cooking over the paltry flames licking at the wood. I guess Walter Rose wanted to do his forest getaway in style.

Milo handed me a marshmallow. I popped it in my mouth. Burnt marshmallow skin crunched under my fangs. The goop stuck to my teeth. I gave them both a thumbs up.

"They're sending a helicopter and a bunch of officers." Walter Rose called from the edge of the camp. "I guess they're not taking any chances." Did he mean for Wambach—or himself? I didn't say any thing and we stayed together, looking at the trees. Rose breathed in the cool fall air. "It's kind of nice out here."

"Yeah," I agreed. "I grew up in these forests. It's nice to visit them."

"But not to live?"

"Nah." I thought back to my current life. Refrigeration, indoor plumbing, fast food, and streaming TV. "I think, for the most part, my people are done with that." I waved to the woods. The trees—and the wolves who had moved back in. "Now, if we can manage not to mess it up, the wilderness belongs to them."

My brother wasn't the one to bring in Wambach, but he knew it was going on. I'd called him up soon after bringing Milo back to the pick-up, now surrounded by a flashing haze of police cars. I talked to the deputies, gave them the short version of what happened, and then we watched the medical helicopter bearing Wambach away. They walked Walter Rose out of there next. No cuffs—he was just a person of interest. Maris stayed with him. A sheriff's deputy would take her back to the winery to get her stuff and wait for her mom to pick her up.

She crossed over to me as her dad settled in the back of the police cruiser. Suspect or not, they were intent on keeping an eye on him. Maris stumbled a little, her boots—without laces—now loose. "I guess I'll say goodbye, Mr. Patches." She nodded to Milo. "I feel bad. I was the one who brought in Dr. Braithwaite. And you."

"You were the only one with pure intentions," I said. "You shouldn't feel guilty."

A shrug. "Will anything good come of it?"

"I don't know." I looked at the trees. "But I'm glad it's over."

She nodded and offered her hand. I shook it and then she stepped into the police car that sped her away.

After that, Milo and I drove straight to Harold's house.

Only a few reporters still lurked around, a deputy's car parked on the curb and keeping them at bay. It was too cold to camp out on the sidewalk or the yard amongst the Halloween decorations, so everyone stayed put.

Rosemary opened the door on the second knock and swept Milo into her arms. Harold, wearing his day-off cardigan, bounded in next and joined the hug. Milo hooted with embarrassment, but still smiled a little as they took turns embracing him.

Then Harold did the same to me. "You kept him safe. Again. Thank you, Porcupine."

I hummed back. "He saved the day himself, just like at Halloween."

They both looked at Milo. "How'd you do that, honey?" Rosemary asked.

He put his hands in his pockets. Behind him, a news station droned on from the TV. They must have had it on, glued to the election returns. Right now, nobody was watching. Milo looked to me and I nodded. "I'm a Singer."

"No." Harold snorted. "That's—that's impossible, son. A myth. Like the Guardian Tree—" He stopped. "Like the Loch Ness Monster."

"That's rich," I said. "Coming from a bigfoot."

But Rosemary, at least, seemed to believe it. "There—there have been reports. I've heard rumors of an alma—the Children of the Earth who come from Russia—in Los Angeles, who claims to be able to talk to plants. It's never been documented, but I suppose there can be some scientific explanation for the frequencies that a sasquatch voice can make and—"

"No." Harold repeated his denial and added a grunt. "Milo, you are a perfectly normal American boy. Do you understand?"

He nodded quietly.

"Squirrel—" I started.

"We'll talk about it later." Harold settled down at the table. The reinforced chair creaked a little under his weight. "Milo, you can go to your room and rest."

"Can I play with my tablet?" he asked.

"Sure." Harold sighed. "You earned it, buddy."

He gave me another look, and then a hug, and then he scampered off.

I decided not to keep arguing—a rare smart decision. Harold had spent his whole life building a respectable and—by human standards—normal life. He colored inside the lines, helped his little sister go to law school and ascend the heights of advocacy, and pulled all the strings he could to keep me out of trouble. Now his only son was a deep forest bigfoot mystic.

It had to hurt.

Rosemary patted his shoulder and started talking with me. "Arlo—why don't you go and say hello to Harriet and Freshta? They're here—and your friends are too."

"My friends?"

Oh no.

I heard the music then, coming from the TV room. *Gucci on a Gator, Balmain on a Bullfrog.*

Burn the forest, it was Stinko and Daisy.

"I'm sorry." I muttered to Rosemary. "I'll run them out."

"Oh, they're no trouble—and we owe them everything for saving your life on Halloween." Rosemary settled in the chair next to Harold. "But can you ask them to turn the music down?"

I went to the living room, but Harriet had beaten me to it. She snatched Stinko's phone out of his hand and switched it to silence, then tossed it back. Her own phone was pressed to her ear, and when Stinko arched his tail and flashed his needle teeth, she held up a single finger to his nose like it was a loaded gun—ending his rage instantly.

Stinko settled back on the couch next to Daisy, who shook her head and patted the humongous stuffed bear sitting next to her. Stinko must have nabbed it from the gift shop after all.

Harriet switched her phone to the next hand. "Sorry about that. No, no—we can still meet. I'd be delighted. How about the Bistro Elegant, tomorrow at around one o'clock?" More conversation. "Yes, by all means. Bring your people. I am very much interested." She switched off the phone. "Mr. Stinko—I am extremely grateful that you saved my life, but do you have to play your music when I'm conducting important SPAC business?"

He smoothed back his mullet. "My bad."

"It certainly is." Her eyes flicked to me. "Hey, Arlo."

"Hey, Treetop." We clasped hands. "Who were you talking to?"

"Hamilton Hamlin."

"You're kidding."

The spoiled scion of HamCo, the energy development company who had employed Lloyd Rusk in the first place. His money was behind everything. He'd be the one selling the timber, extracting the minerals, paving the wilderness, and bringing the scourge of development to Northern California. Why would Harriet be arranging a business lunch with a Harrower like that?

She pocketed the phone. "Hamlin's going to spearhead a new green initiative for HamCo. All renewable and environmentally friendly."

"Can you trust him?" Freshta asked the question from her seat in an armchair in the corner. She still had the machete, in its scabbard, resting across her knees, and her scoped rifle leaning against the wall. Police car outside or not, she was standing guard.

"Not sure—but his money spends, doesn't it?" Harriet said. "He wants to donate a sizeable portion to SPAC."

"And you're going to take it?" I asked.

Stinko let out a snort. "Money makes the human world spin, man. And at least it's for a good cause." He held out his fist to Harriet for a bump. "Go get that bag."

She bumped it. "Sure." Then she gave me a slight smile. "I gotta go get my pitch deck ready. I'll check in soon. How're things looking?"

The TV had switched to commercials. Shambhala Sam himself, advertising new Himalayan Frost breath mints.

"Nothing new," Freshta said.

"Right." She gave my shoulder a nuzzle. "That's how we beat them, Porcupine. We play their game—and we win."

She walked back to the guest room, probably already thinking of what payment plan to drop on Hamilton Hamlin over heirloom tomato salads tomorrow at lunch. I can't say I approved, but I didn't walk in her forest. Harriet was the master there, and I had to accept it.

Freshta reached out and patted her arm as she went by and then looked at me. A respectful nod. Something to a fellow defender. I returned it.

Then I looked back at the TV. Fast food advertisement now.

Stinko was back to flipping through his phone. "Gotta say my goodbyes as well, Arlo."

"Yeah," Daisy agreed. "We'll be motoring out, around tomorrow."

"Where to?" Wherever it was, it wouldn't be boring.

Stinko's smile showed his shimmering gold fangs. "LA, baby."

"That's right," Daisy said. "Stinko's got some deal with an influencer. Wants to start getting his music to a wider audience, turn the Stinko Lifestyle into an actual brand. Sounds silly, I know, but LA's the city for it."

"The Stinko Lifestyle," I repeated. "Aren't you two still wanted for robbery?"

"We'll figure it out," Stinko said. "And I've always wanted to go to Los Angeles. Disneyland. The Hollywood sign. That place with the movie star names on the sidewalk." He patted his belly. "One thing I know about Los Angeles—everyone goes there to make their dreams come true and it always works out."

"Uh-huh." I didn't have the heart to correct him.

"There's just one problem." His joviality faded a little. "I gotta say goodbye to you."

And I would miss him. Strange to say, but for all of Stinko's forest-burning music and braindead ways, he had offered a helping hand when I needed it. I counted him as a friend and I couldn't do that with many in this world, human or bigfoot. I offered my hand and he clasped it while Daisy looked on happily.

"I'll come visit," I said. "Or you come visit."

"Hell yeah," he said. "I do want to come back. I love this place."

The commercial break had ended. We watched as the news chyrons flashed their way across the screen. The ballot counting was coming back. Handy charts showed the progress of candidates and measures. Some races had clear outcomes, but Prop 33 wasn't one of them. Half in favor, half against. Could go either way as the election centers sent in their results.

Rosemary came into the room, bearing snacks. Bowls of dandelion salad sprinkled with bark and drenched in ranch. She passed them around and settled onto the carpet in front of me.

We snacked on salad with our fingers as the news anchors blabbed. "How's Harold and Milo?"

"I talked to him," Rosemary said. "We'll figure out a way for Milo to practice his gifts—safely. And we're still going to give him a normal, happy childhood."

"As normal as can be, for a bigfoot in a human world."

"As normal as that."

New results crept in. The For and Against for Prop 33 was still in a dead heat.

Then something else. Breaking news. "Just in from Nugget County, center of the recently ended occupation of the Charles E. Boles State Park." The anchor's bland face widened in surprise as he read updates off the teleprompter. "Missing real estate magnate and winery owner Walter Rose turned himself into police and is bringing allegations of conspiracy on behalf of well-known Sacramento lobbyist Lloyd Rusk. We go now to our panel of political experts to discuss whether this late-breaking bombshell will change the results of the ongoing election."

Assorted humans in suits looked serious and blathered away.

So Rose was doing his part. But would it matter?

"Might be too late," I said.

"Might be." Rosemary shrugged. "But maybe not."

It all came down to a simple question: what did humans love more? Th trees and the wolves who called them home, or the dream of money in th pockets?

I settled back against the couch and gnawed bark salad, waiting for results to come in. I had high hopes.

Something I've learned working on this case: humans can surprise yo

THE END

www.ingramcontent.com/pod-product-compliance
Lightning Source LLC
LaVergne TN
LVHW010922110826
845149LV00013B/2449

9781969285127